DEGRADATION OF THE WORLD
THE PATH TO IT AND THE PATH OUT OF IT

I SEE FAR™

by

A FRIEND OF MEDJUGORJE

DEGRADATION OF THE WORLD
THE PATH TO IT AND THE PATH OUT OF IT

I SEE FAR™

by

A FRIEND OF MEDJUGORJE

Published with permission from SJP by

CARITAS OF BIRMINGHAM
STERRETT, ALABAMA 35147 USA

No attempt is intended to pre-empt the Church on the validity of the apparitions. They are private revelation awaiting the Church's judgment. Because
the Queen of Peace apparitions are ongoing and not yet over, the Church has
yet to rule on their authenticity. Caritas of Birmingham, the Community of
Caritas and all associated with it, realize and accept that the final authority
regarding the Queen of Peace Medjugorje apparitions rests with the Holy See
in Rome. We at Caritas, willingly submit to that judgment. Caritas of Birmingham and its mission is not connected to the Diocese of Birmingham,
Alabama. The Diocese of Birmingham's official position on Caritas is neutral
and holds us as Catholics in good standing.

— The Publisher

Published with permission from SJP by Caritas of Birmingham

© 1997 SJP
© 2002 SJP
© 2004 SJP
© 2007 SJP
© 2009 SJP
© 2011 SJP

ISBN: 1-878909-07-X

DTTUMAKCTJJJJABC March, 1997

Printed and bound in the United States of America

For additional copies contact your local bookstore or call Caritas of
Birmingham at 205-672-2000, ext. 315 — 24 hours a day.

ABOUT THE AUTHOR

The author of this book is also the author of the books Words From Heaven®, <u>How to Change Your Husband</u>™, <u>I See Far</u>™, <u>Look What Happened While You Were Sleeping</u>™, <u>It Ain't Gonna Happen</u>™ and other publications such as the *Words of the Harvesters* and the *Caritas of Birmingham Newsletter*. He has written more on Medjugorje than anyone in the world, producing life-changing writings and spiritual direction to countless numbers across the world, of all nationalities. He wishes to be known only as "A Friend of Medjugorje." The author is not one looking in from the outside regarding Medjugorje, but one who is close to the events - many times, right in the middle of the events about which he has written; a first-hand witness.

Originally writing to only a few individuals in 1987, readership has grown to over 250,000 in the United States, with additional readers in over one hundred thirty foreign countries, who follow the spiritual insights and direction given through these writings.

The author, when asked why he signs only as "A Friend of Medjugorje," stated:

> *"I have never had an ambition or desire to write. I do so only because God has shown me, through prayer, that He desires this of me. So from the beginning, when I was writing to only a few people, I prayed to God and promised I would not sign anything; that the writings would have to carry them-*

selves and not be built on a personality. I prayed that if it was God's desire for these writings to be inspired and known, then He could do it by His Will and grace and that my will be abandoned to it.

*"The Father has made these writings known and continues to spread them to the ends of the earth. These were Our Lord's last words before ascending: "**Be a witness to the ends of the earth.**" These writings give testimony to that desire of Our Lord to be a witness with one's life. It is not important to be known. It is important to do God's Will."*

For those who require "ownership" of these writings by the author in seeing his name printed on this work in order to give it more credibility, we state that we cannot reconcile the fact that these writings are producing hundreds of thousands of conversions, if not millions through grace, and are requested worldwide from every corner of the earth. The author, therefore, will not take credit for a work that, by proof of the impact these writings have to lead hearts to conversion, have been Spirit–inspired with numbers increasing yearly, sweeping as a wave across the ocean. Indeed in this case, crossing every ocean of the earth. Our Lady gave this author a direct message for him through the visionary, Marija, of Medjugorje, in which Our Lady said to him to witness not with words but through humility. It is for this reason that he wishes to remain simply "A Friend of Medjugorje."

— Caritas of Birmingham

ACKNOWLEDGEMENT

God alone deserves the credit for the publication of
this book. It is from Him that the messages are allowed to be given through Our Lady to all of mankind. He alone deserves the praise and honor.

Special thanks and gratitude to Fred and Carol,
who, through their love and generosity, provided
the grant for the first edition which has perpetuated
the sixth printing of this book. May God reward
them one-hundredfold.

To understand this book fully, please read the following:

The Blessed Virgin Mary is the Mother of Jesus. She is fondly referred to as Our Lady. The Virgin Mary or "Our Lady" began appearing daily to six children in former Yugoslavia on June 24, 1981. Our Lady informed the children that She would be giving messages to the world, as never before since the beginning of man and that these were the last apparitions on earth. The tiny village of Medjugorje began to be transformed through the visits of Our Lady. The Communists, who then ruled former Yugoslavia, to which today's Bosnia and Herzegovina also belonged, were suspicious and persecuted the visionaries. They attempted to stop what can now be considered the most important event since the early beginning of Christianity. People began to flock to the village in massive numbers. News organizations around the world began to take notice as the daily apparitions continued: *Time Magazine, Reader's Digest, Newsweek, Life Magazine, National Geographic, Wall Street Journal*, ABC, NBC, CBS, BBC London and hundreds of others reported about this site and visited it. The village of Medjugorje has now been visited by over 20 million pilgrims, and the fruit of the apparitions is proving it to be the center for **the spiritual renewal for the entire world.** In 1987, Our Lady began to give messages to the world on the 25th of each month. Through various sources, these monthly messages are spread to virtually every inhabited place on earth within hours from the moment Our Lady announces them. These messages are showing the world how to go deeper into the Christian life in a world that is sinking deeper and deeper into sin and evil.

Now 29 years[*] later, all of the visionaries are adults and all are married and having children. Three of the six visionaries still receive daily apparitions. The other three receive apparitions only at certain times during the year. The three who still daily see Our Lady are **Vicka, Ivan, and Marija.** The other three, who no longer see Her daily, but only on special occasions, are Ivanka, Mirjana, and Jakov. Throughout these writings, these visionaries will be quoted.

In January of 1987, Our Lady announced that She is bringing to the world a "plan for the salvation of mankind," especially during these turbulent times. She tells us that we cannot comprehend the greatness of all of our individual roles in this plan. Without a doubt, Medjugorje has changed, is continuing to change, and will forevermore change the world.

These writings are based on the messages given by the Virgin Mary in Medjugorje. When you read bold print with indented sentences in the paragraphs, these are Our Lady's words.

---

[*] This was originally written in 1996. We only updated the year in our reprinting. Often many of these writings are foreseen, even prophetic, by realizing when it was originally written – which the update could make you think it was written in hindsight rather than foresight.

What you are about to read has been prayed about for years. A great deal of discernment through Our Lady's messages and the Holy Spirit has gone into its contents. In our books and newsletters, we have often recommended praying to the Holy Spirit for understanding; however, the following should not even be begun until it can be read slowly, in a contemplative way, and without interruptions. As you read it, become part of it. Find some quiet time or place such as in front of the Blessed Sacrament or some other place of solitude. If you are a Protestant, you may wish to meditate and pray to the Holy Spirit for several moments. If you are not sure of God, pray in your heart to the God you do not know. He will manifest Himself to you. Also, this book was not written to be read one time only. It is to be read several times and each time it is read, you will gain more understanding than the previous reading. It would be wise to put off reading this material until after much prayer. The Holy Spirit will provide the necessary enlightenment and strength to understand, and even to endure, the truth, which was masterfully hidden from us but is now exposed to the light by Our Lady through Her messages. Remember, the following should only be read slowly, after prayer to the Holy Spirit, and from the heart to grasp its full meaning.

TABLE OF CONTENTS

PART ONE
DEGRADATION OF THE WORLD
THE PATH TO IT AND THE PATH OUT OF IT

PART TWO
I SEE FAR™

PART ONE

DEGRADATION OF THE WORLD — THE PATH TO IT AND THE PATH OUT OF IT

*"It has become obvious how the degradation of so-
ciety that took 800 years to sink the Roman Empire
could sink us in one generation."*

*A letter from
Davison, Michigan*

CHAPTER ONE

A MORAL SOCIETY TO AN IMMORAL ONE, HOW DID IT HAPPEN?

Somehow, so deceptively, a whole generation has lost its family values, traditions, and roots. We have gone through an era where everything was questioned, changed or compromised as never before in history. The fabric of what makes up family was redefined and everyone is touched by it. What the family is defined to be today would not only have been abnormal for previous generations but also absurd.

Tragically, the family has become a democracy of individuals with no real direction except that of society. Today's society and culture dictate that the function of a family is to seek as much pleasure and worldly happiness as it wants. To be normal today is to live abnormally in contrast to untold generations before us. Even Christian families have lost the sense of what it really means to live the Christian life. Many are struggling to do so but with <u>everything</u> in society and even things in their homes, such as TV, magazines, etc., contradicting every gain, it seems that it is impossible to live our conversion. How did society end up so far from true Christian life? It's because families quit living the truth. We as a nation (as well as the rest of the world) started to make the decision, several decades ago, that God was no longer part of our lives and should be excluded from society. Many began to assert that God and society were separate, God has nothing to do with government, etc.

How did a God-fearing nation turn away from Him so quickly and lose its spirit of righteousness? We became interested in modern attitudes. satan, so coy, so cunning, masterfully deceived us, and few are able to see what he has done. Our Lady's strongest message has been to pray. Those who have are beginning to realize more and more what is really happening. Indeed, the more we pray, the more we will grasp this book. Everyone would agree satan could not deliver a moral society to its present state without a long-range plan.

Fifty years ago, abortion, murder, corruption, pornography and the multitude of evils plaguing our society would never have been tolerated. Society would have revolted. satan was well aware of this so he seduced us to change our attitudes and our tolerance levels. We became attracted to modern conveniences, going to ball games and the movies. Instead of going fishing with our children, we watched Andy Griffith and Opie go on TV. It was fun, wholesome, exciting and wonderful. Air conditioning took us off the front porch and brought us into the house and made it even more comfortable to sit and watch good shows like "I Love Lucy" on TV. All these things in themselves were not necessarily bad but a great deception was taking place. It was calculated, planned and nurtured over time. We became busier, more engrossed in pleasure, and the television introduced us to a whole new, exciting, fascinating world... And as a fish that sees the worm, eats it, and then realizes to its own demise that it's hooked, we, too, have taken the bait but never even saw the hook. Why?

When we left our back yards and quit spending time with our families on our front porches and became busier and busier, we simply quit praying. Because of this we lost the grace to see the hook. We decided to become reliant on man for our needs and less reliant on God. We were finding answers for everything — vaccines for polio, new materials like plastics, new technology for landing on the moon, new inventions to make life easier — but all the while, life was really getting harder and more complicated. Suddenly many were trying to figure out whether it was better to bring a child into the world to starve or to abort it. TV brought many questions to us, which were very simply and clearly answered a few decades before but had suddenly become so complicated. As gradually as television programming such as "I Love Lucy" and "Andy Griffith" gave way to these things, it also gave way to showing suggestive innocence, kissing scenes, cute things — nothing really objectionable until we realize it desensitized us. After the cutesy scenes came longer sensual kissing scenes, which led to programs like "Peyton Place" and that led to the blatant evil scenes now appearing before us. satan's evil intentions were there all along while he pulled his little red wagon of false innocence.

About the same time we became engrossed in these things and quit praying as a people, we excluded God. We chose man's ideals to form society rather than God's ideals. God gave us what we wanted.

In the Old Testament, the people of Israel wanted a king to rule them instead of the judges but the Prophet Samuel told the people God did not want to give them a king. They still insisted they wanted a king. To the displeased Samuel the Lord said: *"Grant the people's every request. It is not you they reject, they are rejecting me as their king. As they have treated me constantly from the day I brought them up from Egypt to this day, deserting me and worshipping strange gods, so do they treat you too. Now grant their request; but at the same time, warn them solemnly and inform them of the rights of the king who will rule them."* Samuel warned the people of the harm which would come to them and their children but the people refused to listen. They still wanted a king. The Lord said*: "Grant their request and appoint a king to rule them."* Later, they learned first hand how merciless this king was and they suffered greatly because of him. They rejected God's plan to structure their nation and the result was disastrous, causing much bitterness for them.

We are no different from these Israelites. We separated God from our government, our schools, and our institutions and, by doing so, God, respecting our free wills, has allowed us to choose. Now we have inherited a Godless society built by man, fractured with problems and issues that should never have been had we put God first in our lives and prayed. Officials are giving remedies which have not worked and will not work because they exclude God. The answer to all problems is to pray to know the will of God and to do it. **All order, civil, spiritual, and natural, will fall into place when we, as individuals, seek God's will.** We won't get this from television but from prayer. The quagmire the world is in now is because man wanted to do it himself. The world is in such a crisis that God has decided to send Our Lady to pull it out from the path of suicide on which it is headed. Our Lady said:

February 17, 1984

> **"My children, pray! The world has been drawn into a great whirlpool. It does not know what it is doing. It does not realize in what sin it is sinking. It needs your prayers so that I can pull it out of this danger."**

7

"This past year I have 'fallen away' in my prayer, fasting, and devotion to living as our Father urges us through Mary. The results have been my 'falling' into a sinful lifestyle again. Much of this sinfulness is a direct result of what you wrote of in I See Far. As only those who have experienced such awakenings through or by the Holy Spirit can relate to, reading this book was my second 'great call' to renew my passion for a Christian way of life."

A letter from
Cincinnati, Ohio

CHAPTER TWO

NATIONS WILL NOT LEGISLATE SOCIETY'S ILLS AWAY. WHICH PRESIDENT IS ELECTED NO LONGER MATTERS; RATHER ONLY PRAYER!

The world is certainly going in a disastrous direction which is due to man's sins.

We may think, *"Why am I to blame? I don't believe in the acceptance of abortion or illicit-lifestyles."* The truth of the matter is the explosive increase of these sins is the fault of all of us. Through us, these great sins have manifested themselves blatantly! When we quit praying, we became less holy. We may never have been really bad, but we gradually became a less holy people in the Fifties, Sixties and Seventies. Because of the lack of the virtue of holiness, we became more prone to sin even though many of us continued to go to church and most of us considered ourselves okay. Yet, it was not through our committing great sins, but through our lack of holiness, that we as Christians allowed the breeding ground for the great sins of our society. The illicit life-styles who blatantly expose themselves in parades could never do this in an environment of holiness. Unholiness supports them. Our Lady calls us to be light and has said:

March 14, 1985

> **"...I am calling you to the light, which you should carry to all the people who are in darkness. People who are in darkness daily come into your homes. Dear children, give them the light!..."**

Unfortunately our environment is permeated with darkness, but darkness cannot dwell in the presence of light.

Virtually everyone has been influenced by someone in their life who has made an impression on them. In the presence of someone who is holy, we are on our best behavior. Their light, their holiness, inspires us toward this. Their witness is powerful enough to cause change and suppress darkness. What swearer curses in the presence of Mother Teresa?

No politician, no government is going to remedy any of our present problems. **WE ARE,** through Our Lady and Her messages. The world spends billions for programs to remedy our problems — drugs, crime, teenage pregnancy, AIDS, etc. Politicians offer answers, which would fill up the world's libraries and yet we have the answer to all these problems. It is very simple. The answer to drugs is holiness; to teenage pregnancy, holiness; to AIDS, holiness. The answer is very simple, and we must uncomplicate things and just be holy. Our Lady said:

December 25, 1989

"...For years I have been calling you to encourage you to a profound spiritual life in simplicity,..."

Through our living a life of holiness, Our Lady commissions us to bring something wonderful to the whole world, something for which the whole world yearns, something for which the very heart of man is craving. We are to rejoice because it will come from God through us for the world. Our Lady said:

June 24, 1992

"...You are the ones who will bring peace to the world."

We have toyed with so many new things and accepted them, never having the foresight that they would lead to the destruction of the family and society. Not having this wisdom was the fruit of not praying. We didn't pray because we were more fascinated with the TV, etc. Our Lady said:

11

July 30, 1987

> **"...Children, darkness reigns over the whole
> world. People are attracted by many things and
> they forget about the more important..."**

The human race is in grave danger, headed for disastrous ruin. Our Lady goes to the extreme and says there is only one way to save it from its present direction. She said:

July 30, 1987

> **"...Prayer is the only way to save the human
> race."**

The world is in a tangle and it cannot get free on its own. It is being strangled by its own doing. However, God, in His mercy, will help us. This can be compared to a little boy playing with his mother's ball of yarn. First, he slowly toys with it but gets more and more tangled in it. While struggling to get free from it, he becomes more tangled and endangers himself with strangulation. Hearing him choking, his mother runs to his rescue but cannot free him immediately because of the risk of choking him further and doing permanent harm. So she works with all the speed, patience, intensity and concern she can, delicately untangling this string and severing another, detaching the strings one by one with a steady hand until she gets to the string around his neck and frees him. The child saw absolutely no danger in the ball of yarn and, in fact, couldn't have seen the potential danger.

Just as the mother came to her child's rescue, Mary is sent to the world which is choking with sin. The family is so entangled that to make any rapid moves would run the risk of breaking up the family and causing more harm. So with intensity, concern, patience, and speed, Our Lady delicately begins freeing us from the stranglehold of the society man has built, knowing all the while if the process moves too quickly it will rupture relationships. In Her wisdom, She initiates our formation through prayer and, in this way, She slowly frees us. There are casualties along the way because of obstinate hearts who refuse the grace to change and make a clean break with the direction in which the world is going, yet others go forward. It is a tragedy for those who stay behind and "die" (rejecting Our Lady's plan) during the process just as it would be for the patient who dies on the operating table. It is the reason Our Lady said Jesus offers us a way which is bitter; but through this bitterness we will discover sweetness by getting rid of the petty things in our lives which will open our hearts to be changed.

July 25, 1987

> **"...Dear children, pray and accept all that God is offering you on a way which is bitter. But at the**

same time, God will reveal every sweetness to whomever begins to go on that way, and He will gladly answer every call of God. Do not attribute importance to petty things..."

Yet when a family commits to Our Lady, the way will be sweet and joyful. Our Lady said:

August 5, 1985:

"...Give your utmost and we will go together, sensitive to the sweetness of life, light, and joy..."

What must we do to change our direction? First of all, reject those things which led us onto this path.

The Bible speaks of a time in the end when there will be a great increase of knowledge in man, but they will know nothing. It is difficult to see how anyone who is in a spirit of prayer cannot see that we are in such times, with schools and universities corrupting the minds of the youth. We can begin to understand why St. Francis refused to allow his people to be educated by institutions of his day. We must show the same concern St. Francis showed. The test we must pass is that of Holiness. It is the reason we are put here on the Earth. All else is trivial and means nothing in the end. satan wants to drive us far from Christian life and will do everything to make us think our job, our home, our financial security is important. In reality, these things mean nothing...absolutely nothing, because passing the test of Holiness during this brief moment of life will prove at our graduation of this life into the next to be the only test which mattered. All else of the world is fruitless...

September 25, 1992

"...In a 'special way,' he (satan) wishes to destroy your souls. He wishes to guide you as far away as possible from Christian life as well as from the commandments, to which the Church is calling you, so you may live them. satan wishes to destroy everything which is holy in you and around you. Therefore, little children, pray, pray, pray..."

We cannot just empty ourselves and not refill. It is a mistake to think, *"Okay, I'll quit doing everything unholy."* This is only half the process. We must replace these things with holy acts and deeds and live holiness by our very lives, because our families, friends, nation, and the world will depend on our witness for eternity.

PART TWO

I SEE FAR™

*"After reading <u>I See Far</u>, everything is clear. I
have for years had the feeling or knowledge that
the world is <u>way out of control and way off bal-
ance</u> when it comes to God and living according to
His ways. There is such a monstrous difference
between the way I was taught and the way the
people of today think. I often wonder what happened to the people who were brought up as I was.
Where are they? Doesn't anyone think about God
and the Commandments as Sacred and Holy anymore? I have often thought that it can't go on this
way much longer. God is going to have to do
something."*

*A letter from
Hilbert, Wisconsin*

CHAPTER THREE

THE GREAT CRIME!

Seeing where this book leads may be almost unbearable; therefore, some may wish to deny the following. Nevertheless, with Our Lady and following the steps of Her messages and the logic contained within them, inflamed by the Holy Spirit, the truth will come forth in any heart who seeks it. Upon completing this, it will be much easier to understand why Our Lady said:

April 4, 1985

> **"...I wish to keep on giving you messages as it has never been in history from the beginning of the world..."**

Coming upon the crime scene, the detective knew nothing. As he began the work of investigating, it soon became evident he was dealing with a premeditated crime and the perpetrator and motive behind it were masterfully concealed. With all crimes, evidence exists and soon, with hard work, small, infinitesimal pieces of information began to add up. Alone, these shreds of evidence meant nothing — a footstep in the dirt, a piece of clothing, etc. — but added together, they began to reveal more and more truth. Each item, like a piece of a puzzle, showed nothing, but once put together, the full picture could be seen. With all the evidence collected, it was easy for the detective to see the truth and know who was guilty.

Something has happened in the world today which has been masterfully concealed. A crime of such magnitude that many pieces of the puzzle from so many different sources must be brought together to even begin to see the picture. However, once collected, assembled, and combined with an open heart, the jolting truth becomes clear that we on earth have been so masterfully deceived.

In the Book of Job, we read how satan appeared before the throne of God and conversed with God. He made a request to God, Who granted his request to test His holy Job for a time. satan tried to make Job turn from God by putting him through many tests.

One day Pope Leo XIII, after celebrating Holy Mass, was in conference with some cardinals and he suddenly sank to the floor. A physician who was nearby thought he was dead as he felt no pulse. However, he did come to and with great emotion he said: *"Oh, what a horrible picture I have been permitted to see."* [1] What Pope Leo saw was satan talking to God, and he heard the voice of satan asking God for a time with the Church, just as satan did in the Scriptures with Job. Pope Leo heard satan ask for a century in order to turn the Church from God, and his request was granted. The Pontiff had this vision toward the end of the 19th century, and it cannot be discounted that satan and God may have had this conversation centuries or even a thousand years before. No one can be certain; however, it was stated to Pope Leo that the 19th and 20th century is satan's and spanning back 60 centuries, it would be extremely difficult to defend that it has not belonged to him. When one considers Scripture — that satan requested Job and God granted it — could we possibly not believe it also for God to grant a century to satan?

The visionary, Mirjana, related that satan appeared to her and tried to tempt her to **renounce** Our Lady. When Mirjana rejected him, Our Lady immediately appeared to her and said:

Before December 26, 1982

> **"Excuse me for this, but you must realize that satan exists. One day he appeared before the throne of God and asked permission to submit the Church to a period of trial. God gave him permission to try the Church for one century. This century is under the power of the devil, but when the**

secrets confided to you come to pass, his power will be destroyed. Even now he is beginning to lose his power and has become aggressive. He is destroying marriages, creating division among priests and is responsible for obsessions and murder. You must protect yourselves against these things through fasting and prayer, especially community prayer. Carry blessed objects with you. Put them in your house, and restore the use of holy water."

With our limited intelligence, we want as much time as possible to prepare for any major task or feat we wish to accomplish. It is with simple logic that a far superior intellect would have enough sense to conclude the same. Perhaps for a long time, satan planned and schemed all his deceptions, as carefully as a criminal, to cover his tracks and to hide all evidence to capture man, who was totally unaware. Small pieces of evidence show up even in the late 1800's of his preparations and plans to dominate and control the events of this century. Perhaps Our Lady is appearing in the latter part of this century in preparation for the next century, to take what satan has amassed and destroy it as we go into the next century during which She will reign and dominate.

"I have been reading I See Far. It was very hard to accept at first, but the more I read the more I began to see that many of these thoughts have run through my mind long before I read this. I pushed them aside, thinking I was getting a little bit odd in my old age, but now I see God has been speaking to me all along, trying to get my attention. I See Far gave me just that — the ability to see far. Everyone must read this. It will be a priority for me to help everyone in my family see now what I see. Thanks!"

A letter from
Orlando, Florida

CHAPTER FOUR

THE THEFT OF MAN; THE INSTRUMENT
USED FOR THE CRIME

If we accept what the Pope heard, what the visionaries of Medjugorje say, and many other things as proof that satan had been given power in the world as never before, it is reasonable that he would follow simple concepts. The Pied Piper story contains all the elements he needs to entice and mesmerize people into following him. Just as the Pied Piper allured, entranced and entertained the mice into following him right into the water to their death by drowning, so, too, is satan's desire to cleverly lead people, without a hint of their impending danger, to spiritual death. What would be necessary? The Pied Piper had his pipe. satan would have to come up with his creation. He would also have to have a trap, a net, which would take a lot of work to ensnare all the people together; but once captured, they could be **"net-worked"** together to listen to his pipe so he could lead them. One rotten apple in a bushel basket will spoil those next to it, and those, in turn, would further infect those surrounding them. Space between the apples would slow or stop this process. This master intellect understood clearly that without a network tying all people together, his plan to infect every man possible would become too difficult. So the concept of networking and the ideals in the Pied Piper story were the foundation upon which everything would be formed. Would not the father of witchcraft desire a **medium** through which to speak? Webster defines "medium:"

> **Medium:** a go between, intermediary, an individual held to be a channel of communication between the earthly world and a world of spirits.[2]

This medium, in order to deceive man and be able to lead him astray, would offer good, pleasurable enlightenment and, in so doing, seduce him to ruin later, after having led him astray. But would these things of his century be ideals, spiritual concepts or actual physical things of his creation?

Fortunately for us, but not the case with the mice, man is blessed with Our Lady's appearances just as satan is leading us into the water to drown. She, through Her messages, began to tell us that we have been deceived. *"No,"* we responded, *"the music is beautiful and we're being entertained."* Our Lady relayed through Her messages that we've been entranced. *"No,"* we responded, *"the things the piper offers us are good."* Our Lady said there are evil things and She began to explain gently and slowly. Many who responded to Our Lady and Her messages realized we had been masterfully duped as were the mice. What has Our Lady been saying? What has She been exposing?

It is important to realize that the people of former Yugoslavia, to which Bosnia and Herzegovina with Medjugorje also belonged, lived under the terrorism and oppression of Communism. The evils of Communism, so close at hand, would be one of the many things we might expect Our Lady to have mentioned but She never did. Abortion, listed as the number-one evil in the world on many people's list, has never been mentioned by Our Lady in a public message. Understanding this, those remaining things, which Our Lady does mention, must be considered with great importance. When we examine Our Lady's messages, it is extremely rare that She mentions a **physical thing,** and it is even more rare that She mention this "thing" more than once. However, one thing Our Lady mentioned on several occasions, and even in a message to the world, is some "thing" we live with daily, ignoring its bad qualities because of its "perceived" good qualities. It is so rooted into the fabric of our lives that its influence is no longer seen as a danger to our spiritual lives for eternity. There is only one physical **"thing"** which Our Lady tells us to **<u>AVOID</u>** in over sixteen years of apparitions (as of June, 1997). She uses the word "avoid" and She Herself specifically ties this word directly and unmistakably to a material object. She said:

June 16, 1983

"Avoid television."

Once more, this was given as a rule for the purpose of growing in the spiritual life. Television is the single "thing" which Our Lady has specifically mentioned and spoken about several times. She went as far as telling us it is of **no value** and to **renounce** it. Our Lady wants us to restart and change from this moment. She "plainly" states "clearly" so that no one can misunderstand: **"Turn off the television"** and let Lent be the incentive to do this because this weekly message for the world was given in the beginning of Lent. She does not mean to do it only for Lent. Lent is only the incentive. When we change, we must not go back to our old ways or we can never say we've changed.

February 13, 1986

> **"Dear children, this Lent is a special incentive for you to change. Start from this moment. Turn off the television and renounce various things of no value..."**

"Change," "start," "turn off," "renounce." It is of great significance that Our Lady has never mentioned the great sins and atrocities of our time and yet boldly and strongly says to

"renounce things" of **no value** and names **"television"** as the first example. It is first among the **"things"** to renounce. One may think, *"I do not care much for TV but occasionally I may watch it."* Our Lady is telling us something about which we may not have been fully conscious: She wants it out of our lives. The definition of renounce:

> **Renounce:** to give up by formal declaration, to refuse to follow, obey, or recognize any further.[3]

Our Lady could not in any way have meant only during Lent because it is a contradiction to come back to what you have renounced as it is defined in the dictionary. And if this is true in regard to secular life, then what does renounce mean in the spiritual life? She said to start from this moment to change. Change and do what? The word "renounce" carries great importance; its meaning is clear, with no gray line of compromise that maybe Our Lady only means for us to partially turn away. The word is too strong to minimize it to mean something less than what it says. satan certainly knows the word "renounce," for he himself appeared to Mirjana in order for her to renounce Our Lady (as you've already read on page 21). So it is now Our Lady appears in an opposite way and tells us to renounce the television. Our Lady associates "renounce" to television through several of Her messages but also uses the word to apply it to that which the TV leads: bad thoughts and desires, materialism, etc. Our Lady says:

29

February 22, 1988

✓ "...Renounce sin..."

Can it be by chance that She has used the word "renounce" for both **sin** and for **television**? Is that in itself a message? A survey reported[4] that when people were asked how much money it would take for them to give up television for life, many reported great sums and 20% said for no amount would they renounce it. This attachment to a "thing" tells of something in man that is fundamentally wrong. Our Lady tells us to renounce that thing which we like the most.

December 15, 1989

✓ "...Renounce some 'thing' that you like most."

There is something much more behind television which causes it to be the one "thing" of the world Our Lady specifically recommends and invites us to renounce.

"Our Lady of Medjugorje called for a year of the youth a few years ago. Later the Pope called for a year of the youth. Later, Our Lady called for a year of the family. Later, yet again, the Pope called for the year of the family. Next Our Lady called to renounce television, beginning in Lent of 1986. A few weeks after the tenth anniversary of Our Lady's message, Pope John Paul II, at the beginning of Lent called for a fast from TV. Many were shocked. Italian TV, with networks around the world, broadcasted his statement from his balcony. He said along with his request:

'In families, the television seems to substitute rather than facilitate dialogue among people.'

It seems the Pope's thinking merges with the Virgin Mary's, by the power of the Holy Spirit!"

Associated Press, Monday, March 11, 1996,
an eyewitness account in Italy

CHAPTER FIVE

CAN "THINGS" BE EVIL?

One father who began to see what Our Lady was saying had given a great deal of thought about TV for many months: the damage, the perceived good, etc. One day in prayer he concluded that he and his children would destroy it. He reasoned it out for an hour while in prayer and committed to renounce it officially and destroy it. In the last minute of the hour of prayer, having already decided what and even how to do it, the practical thought sprang upon him: *"Wait a minute. The TV is just a box. It's a thing. Things are not evil. I just can't be a kook and think this way. Perhaps I am reacting in extremism."* He put the thought aside, knowing to act in extremism was wrong except in his love for God. Two days later, he awaited, as he does each month, for Our Lady's message on the 25th of the month to be announced. When it was he was amazed how almost directly She confirmed his discernment.

August 25, 1992

> **"...I call upon you to open yourselves completely to me, so that through each of you I may be enabled to**

33

convert and save the world, where there is much sin and <u>many 'things'</u> which are <u>evil</u>...."

He immediately realized that the "practical" thoughts which sprang upon him were not of God and that it was the Holy Spirit who had prompted his first contemplation. Two days later, Our Lady's message confirmed with clear words that, yes, there are **things** which are evil. From this he determined to carry out formally and officially his renouncement and did so afterwards.

Many times Our Lady has referred to the word, "things" in Her messages. While this includes many items, it is to Her messages we must go to see what material things of the world She has mentioned. The **TV** is the example; it holds the first place, being named directly among the things about which She has spoken. When you read Our Lady's message, you'll see the word, "thing," can first be applied to television. Even though Our Lady mentions television on several occasions, She sometimes uses simply the word "thing." The word, "television," and the word, "thing," swap out in almost all cases. It is obvious it holds the first place among the things about which She is referring. Through Her messages, you'll see how our attachment to this is so strong that it kills the spiritual life. When speaking of this, Our Lady again uses the words, "renounce" and "things" (television). She said:

Can "Things" Be Evil?

February 25, 1990:

> **"...I especially want you to <u>renounce</u> all the things to which you are attached but are <u>hurting your spiritual life</u>. Therefore, little children, decide completely for God, and do not allow satan to come into your life through those things that hurt both you and your spiritual life..."**

Our Lady asks us to renounce all the things to which we are attached and are hurting us and our spiritual lives. Ask yourself, *"What is the foremost thing which can do this?"* It is a dominating and guiding force over the whole world's population. Our Lady does not want us to obey a voice from the opposite direction any longer but to listen to Her voice.

June 16, 1983

> **"...Have them not listen to him (satan), nor obey him. It is to the voice of the Blessed Virgin that they should pay attention...."**

Our Lady is coming with Her voice, and Her message is in direct opposition to satan's voice and his message. Our Lady wants to help us and make us aware of satan's deception and uncover that voice which he has put right in our midst. Our

Lady wants the truth known about this "thing" which is being used to prevail over and in our hearts:

September 25, 1986

> **"...I am calling you, so that by your prayer and your life you help to destroy everything that's evil in people and <u>uncover</u> "the deception" that satan makes use of. You pray that the truth prevails in all hearts...."**

Uncover what? satan makes use of what? We know what sin is: murder, adultery, theft, gossip, slander, jealousy, etc. Why does Our Lady end the above message with, *"that the truth prevails in all hearts?" What is it that we don't "see?"* Perhaps because we are so preoccupied with "this thing," She knows when we are turned to the TV, we cannot be turned to the Holy Spirit, and He cannot work in us.

May 9, 1985

> **"...Your hearts are turned toward the <u>things</u> of earth and they preoccupy you. Turn your hearts toward prayer and seek the Holy Spirit to be poured out on you..."**

However, we respond, *"I pray and can do that after I watch some programs."* Our Lady makes no bones about this. In the very beginning months of Her apparitions, She says you cannot do both.

December 8, 1981

> **"...It would be a good thing to give up television, because after seeing some** (one or several) **programs, you are distracted and unable to pray..."**

Many may respond, *"this is too hard. Why can't we see a little? Perhaps we can at least see the news and read the newspaper. After all, one must be informed."* Our Lady says:

April 17, 1986

> **"If you look at the programs, if you look at the newspapers, your heads are filled with news, then there is no longer any place for me in your hearts..."**

It is easy to reject the above message and discount that Our Lady doesn't really mean that literally, yet, this message was given to the prayer **group and they themselves questioned Our Lady's advice** regarding watching television and reading newspapers as too difficult. She responded with the above words when they complained, after having already told them not to watch TV. But still, the question lingers. We want to be informed! Fr. Frank Poncelet, in his book, Air Waves From Hell, writes four rationalizations people use to justify why they must watch TV. His third rationalism addresses those who feel they must be informed. He writes:

> **Statement:** Third Rationalization: TV is a necessary tool for information so that people can be in touch with the world...
>
> **Answer:** With the world, right? That is the whole question. TV sells you the world like the devil did when he tempted Christ. TV is intrinsically worldly, materialistic, and humanistic. It can only say, "the world is the world is the world. That's all there is and that's good enough." It trains us not to see God's hand, yet, while man should be informed about the society in which he lives, true; but what you see on TV, however, is not the truth. It is altered, manipulated, and that's not how you should inform yourself.[5]

An executive producer from one of the three major networks relayed: *"We produce shows, news documentaries, to let the viewer 'feel' they've been treated fairly and objectively and then we can lead them in to what we want them to believe in the end."* [6]

While presently there are just a few people who recognize these things, through Our Lady's messages, there is a growing knowledge among Her children that something is fundamentally wrong regarding the television, and these few are beginning to do something about it. October, 1990, the Balthasar House was opened in Rome, Italy, to prepare young men for a life of evangelical consecration. Pope John Paul II was presented their charter by Cardinal Ratzinger. Their charter, the contract each member must sign, includes, *"There will be no television set in the house."* It adds, *"we joyfully give up much that the world considers normal and make rare use of other forms of the mass media."* [7] But what if one avoids evil programs and commercials and watches only good shows and commercials then, ask yourself, for what reason does the Balthasar House expel it altogether?

Finally this chapter raises the issue of the theological aspect: that God made all of creation, therefore, all is good. Some have mistranslated the August 25, 1992 message in different languages to sanitize it, to be "theologically in tune." However, Our Lady's messages must be understood in light of all Her messages. She well knows all creation is of God, and therefore, the things from the Creator cannot be evil. A gun can be used for good or evil — hunting to provide for one's self or robbery to provide one's greed. This, therefore, cannot be said this "thing" (gun) is evil. The laws of physic, in the way it operates and the elements it is made from is of God's creation, therefore, not evil. However, the equation is now before modern man of the derivative he (man) has made from God's creation — that are things which are evil. What is the purpose of the most common birth control device? Lay these items on a table. For the Christian who understands, it is an evil thing. Yes, it is made from God's elements found in creation, but which were never intended for such violations of God's natural law. The Atomic Bomb cannot be claimed as evil. It saved many lives, even Japanese, when they had vowed to fight to the last man. But what of the R-42 Abortion pill? It is an evil thing with only one purpose. Yes, the Atomic Bomb kills and the R-42 pill kills, but one still cannot be classed as an evil thing, while the other can be classed as intricately evil and a disturbance of God's creation birthed by man's creation. It is difficult to find anything that could be described as an evil thing before the eve of modern technology, but now the world is beginning to accumulate things which have no value except as evil. Human cloning and the genetic reordering of man are only a few among many of the intrinsically evil things man has created through derivatives of God's creation. His is holy, man's is evil (technology and development against natural law).

Lastly, what about the tree of good and evil that God made in the Garden of Eden? It cannot be said it was intricately evil, for its purpose was for man to show his love for God through it by obedience of not eating of it. Things today which are evil, at the very least, should be dealt with, at least as the same. Much more so that they are creations of man's unbridled search to become masters of his own destiny. The result is disaster after disaster of society and its deterioration. There are things in our modern world which are evil, for they have no purpose to exist other than to exist to violate God's natural law.

"It has been a wonderful year of change in our family as we read and live the words Our Lady has been sending us. The improvements in our lives have been tremendous as the television has been turned off and the caring for one another has become the most important aspect of our lives. We now see more clearly with adult vision the invasion that television has brought into our home and the disruption of family living. We are thankful for the insight and harmony provided by your book."

*A letter from
South Bend, Indiana*

CHAPTER SIX

WORDS TELL MARY'S INTENTIONS
WORDS TELL THE MEDIUM'S INTENTIONS

Our Lady didn't say to partially give up television.
What She wants from us is something much stronger than going
part way. Our Lady says, **"avoid."** Avoid means: **expel; to
depart or withdraw from; leave; to keep away from.**[8]

June 16, 1983

> **"Renounce all passions and all inordinate desires.
> Avoid television, particularly evil programs,…"**

Again, renounce shows up in the same message with television
and now, knowing the full meaning of **"avoid,"** it seems that this
would be a word you would use for an exorcism — Expel?
Withdraw from? Leave? If this century belongs to satan, is it
possible his influence so dominates all the earth, even Christians,
that Her call is for something like an exorcism? Is the television
the instrument created to lead man like the Pied Piper did with
his pipe? It is strange that after years of Our Lady's being with
us, and after years during which many are praying and trying to

do what She asks, that as recently as July 25, 1993, we receive a message in which She says:

July 25, 1993

> **"...I do not want satan to deceive you, for he wants to lead you the wrong way..."**

We are Her children. We don't want satan to deceive or lead us astray either. If we are going to Holy Mass and saying our prayers, what is Our Lady talking about — that satan wants to lead us astray? What is the television? What does it do to us? What possible harm can come from watching good shows? It is important to go back to the very first hour of this century, the first hour of satan's time which we might call it if this century belongs to satan. What is recorded about that hour? What would that hour be called? That first hour which birthed a new dawn for a new century? Irving Settel in his book, <u>A Pictorial History of Television</u>, writes:

> *"In New York at the **witching hour** of midnight, December 31, 1899, horns blew and champagne flowed in a celebration seldom **matched for frantic joy.** This was no ordinary New Year's Eve along Broadway from Union Square to 42nd Street. Silk-hatted men, **bejeweled** women at Del Monico's, Sherry's, and Hammerstein's Paradise Roof Garden danced*

*and drank to a new century. The change of the Number from 18 to 19 struck the spark. To America, the Twentieth Century meant hope, progress, a fabulous future for a **lusty** nation. Everything **modern** acquired the label, '**20th Century.'** Everything prior to 1900 became suddenly 'Victorian.' If you were not '20th Century' in dress, deportment, and **daring,** you were old hat."* [9]

Witching hour, bejeweled women, frantic joy, dancing, drinking, lusty, modern, and daring would be a good description of someone who believed satan had just been given the century; however, the source quoted is purely secular. He was completely unaware of the points he showed and the cause of celebration by breaking away from the past 60 centuries to the freedom of the new world of the 20th Century. It was the rush to bring an instrument into the world to pipe a tune which causes breakthrough after breakthrough to happen.

Researching the birth of television through secular sources, one will find repeatedly the words, "miracle" and "miraculous," used. One source writes that when the human voice was carried over wire that it was an ***"invented authentic miracle."*** [10] The dawn of this century is described as *a "period of swift technological advances."* [11] What suddenly catapulted men and technology? Scanning secular sources, you'll find descrip-

45

tions of miraculous, accidental breakthroughs, things invented but not with the real understanding of how they worked, so the word magical was used often to describe their function such as in the following:

> *"It is purely electronic magic, something strange in the world and to thoughtful people rather frightening."* [12]

Again, a secular source even describes television as "strange in the world," and even frightening, not to ignorant people but to thoughtful people. Could this truly be an instrument with the express purpose to captivate man, so much so that thoughtful men had the discernment that something was disturbing about it? More evidence and pieces of the picture are found when we look at the words which are used for TV. They contain several elements of witchcraft and are main clues to show that perhaps Our Lady is upon the earth to uncover a deception. The Pictorial History of Television describes television *as "modern wizardry."* [13] It is referred to in all sources, both secular and religious, as a **medium/media.** The meaning of **"medium"** has already been explained as a go-between, an **intermediary,** connecting the world of earth to the world of spirit. A spiritualist is a medium for channeling different spirits and this can be achieved through different **channels.** These words, when viewed as shown, cast the "medium" as the "anti" of Our Lady spiritually coming to speak Her words to us.

"Today my eyes, mind, and heart have been opened as never before — I just finished reading your book I See Far. Each newsletter or book you send is wonderful — but this one was so special regarding the TV. I have turned it off and it will not be turned on again. I can't believe how so many of us were 'taken in' — myself most of all."

A letter from
North Haven, Connecticut

CHAPTER SEVEN

WHAT HAPPENS WHEN ALL
CULTURES BECOME THE SAME?

A plan of massing everyone together to infect all is also achieved through the capturing of all minds underneath this medium, TV, network. Just as fish are caught in a net, you can see when flying over communities in a small plane, all homes are tied together by air waves or cables. Regardless of culture, tradition, or heritage, all homes and institutions are tied together with those of other towns, cities, states and countries throughout the whole world. This network is the great achievement, and parallels the one, small, insignificant, rotten apple which can spread its rot throughout a whole basket of fruit. How is it that so many of the youth and adults of the world with their radically different cultural backgrounds are all falling into the same patterns, the same fad: family breakdowns, divorce, murder, suicide, depression, and immorality? In contrast, on an island where TV is barred, a study showed the youth of the island to be the most complete, joyful, happy, balanced youth anywhere in the world.[14] Then how is it that people of the earth with diverse backgrounds are plagued with the same patterns of problems already mentioned; and where TV is barred, the people, especially the youth, are radically different? It seems the TV itself is the means for its own message, even dictating its own lifestyles and patterns for man to imitate.

Searching the evidence several decades back, the thought from many sources was that what the TV gives is "a message." Recently, however, most all secular sources refer to it as *"the medium 'is' the message."*[15] The author of the introduction of Pictorial History of Television states:

> *"It has taken a super-sophisticated triumph of man's insatiable curiosity and ingenuity to restore the message of mankind to its most primitive form."* [16]

While he may be speaking of communication, man's most primitive form was based in idolatry and TV is stated in the quote as the means to achieve it. It is not someone who is a religious who states this, rather a former CBS executive who is pro-TV. What would be behind a move of restoration (or resurrection) to bring man back to his primitive form? What is behind it obviously has its own message, and it counters Our Lady who has Her message. Which do we choose, satan and his deceptive strength, or Our Lady and Her love for us? Because of that love, shouldn't we believe Her and Her words? Our Lady tells us to decide.

November 25, 1987

"...Pray that satan does not entice you with his pride and deceptive strength. I am with you and I want you to believe me that I love you..."

The television produces prodigies that are wonders. It can show incredible things and imagery, such as earthquakes, the dead rising, and even fire coming down from the heavens. Yes, it is deceptive and not real but many are deceived and even lose a sense of reality. One small five-year-old took his father's gun, went into the kitchen, and killed his mother.[17] He did not understand why she did not get back up after seeing the TV stars get shot and reappear on the next week's series. One might think only children are deceived but these writings will show that adults are included as well.

One other word of importance to trace, in order to understand television, is the word itself. The iconoscope, invented in the beginning of this century, was called the eye because of exactly what it did. It duplicated the human eye for the TV camera, an outstanding breakthrough. So many of the inventions for TV mechanically parallel human functions. Therefore, it is easy to trace and see that these things which have no life, duplicate that which is life and when made up into instruments can be of great danger to man. This was the case with Eve. She did not realize the danger because her eyes were deceived,

51

because of desire and disobedience. The television is often referred to in some sources as an eye. But it is our own eyes we lend to it to be seduced. It was through the eye that the serpent brought down man the first time, and now a second time, he pulls the whole world in his grip through the eye. The first time the serpent tells Eve:

Genesis 3:5–6

> *"No, God knows well that the moment you eat of it your __eyes__ will be opened.... The woman __saw__ that the tree was good for food and pleasing to the __eye__ and desirable for gaining wisdom."*

All this perfectly describes television — entertaining food for the mind, pleasing and desirable to the eye, and, all the while, supposedly enlightening us with wisdom — all through the eye. After both Adam and Eve ate of the fruit, the Scripture says:

> *"Then the eyes of both of them were opened."*

They could suddenly see what they could never see before. They could "see far" into things when before they were kept innocently pure and protected by the Father. They saw nakedness for the first time. Before that, they were naked but sensuality did not exist. There was no perversion of the body. The "apple" changed that, just as television now is increasing and spreading the same. Is the purpose of television the same? Is the serpent, most cunning of all creatures, not duplicating man's fall through the eye during the 19th and 20th century, as he did to Adam and Eve hundreds of centuries before? The word, "television," itself gives more evidence to help us make up our minds. Two languages which may be said to have been used for holy use were Greek and Latin. Many translations from the Bible came from the Greek language. Latin, of course, was the language of the Church for ages. Possessed people who know nothing of the language often spew out perfect vocabulary in Latin. satan always uses that which is God's in his action of opposing God. It is not proper to mix two root words from different languages, yet, the word, television, does just that. No one is quite sure what force brought about a word which offends scholars and linguists. However, its meaning may help you discern what is perhaps not traceable on a human level. The meaning is the same thing told to Eve.

> *Tele/vision: the Greek root, **"tele,"** means far. The Latin root, **"video,"** means **"I see."** Far I see, or once properly formed to its clear meaning, "I see far."* [18]

The serpent's promise was "your eyes will be opened," (far you'll see). Indeed, in the last and now this century, our eyes have been opened, our innocence and even that of our children is gone, because now "we see far" by the television. Perhaps in a different degree, but the same thing was offered to Eve. Is it a vision? An evil vision of the last and this century? The voice Eve heard? And to crush it, does God now send Our Lady? Is this why Our Lady specifically mentions this medium and refers to it — something She has not done except only rarely concerning material things specifically? Most words when changed into other languages are very different. For instance, the word "can opener" can differ greatly from language to language. Strangely though, the word, television, is universally spelled and pronounced almost the same way in every language. Is it by chance that this word is the same in every language? Collect the following words in prayer: **magical, electronic wizardry, prodigies, medium/media, TV channel(ing), network, message, the eye, television.** Is this making too much over too little? Perhaps one could say that looking only at this aspect; however, all the pieces must be put together, and indictments made by the evidence itself, considering these words along with other evidence. Small pieces of evidence are in themselves minimal and mean little until all wedded together and the full picture is seen. The deception taking place does just that, "deceives." The perpetrator destroys whatever evidence he can and keeps the rest of the evidence hidden or fragmented so there is no notice of what really took place or is taking place. Some crimes take place in view of many, others only under cover or darkness. Could it be that this is perpetrated in view of everyone, in the light, undetected?

"I do agree with you that we should avoid looking at television for it destroys some of our community life. We have no evening recreation any more since three years. My reaction was to stop looking at television. Some of the other sisters do also, but not all of them."

A letter from a nun
in Angers, France

CHAPTER EIGHT

A PRIEST DISCOVERS THE TRUTH

The Church fathers tell us, *"The eyes are the windows of the soul."* If protected, innocence dwells; and if exposed to the world, filth dwells.

Fr. Al Winshman, S.J., who has been active for years in the Medjugorje Movement was interviewed by Caritas of Birmingham regarding television, his giving it up, and why.

Question: *Do you think television is dangerous for the family structure? We've gone thousands of years without something like this. Then suddenly this comes on man's horizon and forms his whole thought pattern and his opinions. It's actually a direction, and, of course, a direction in a spiritual sense as a spiritual director would direct. Could this be something that's just too dangerous to have within the family? In other words, families for thousands of years had to deal with boredom, had to deal with what they were going to do in the evening and now we've got this...*

Father: *Right. You don't have the social events. What I experienced in my own life immediately, when I made the decision back in the fall of '84 that television couldn't be my habitual way of winding down at night, — I suddenly had all kinds of time to do some good reading, to talk with people that I never had a chance to before. It was just a whole different quality of life which began to develop almost overnight, to say nothing about the five or six years later when I began to reflect back on what effects this had had on my life. I singled out three primary areas that I think are destroying our culture, certainly here in America.*

1. Materialism was one. I noticed without being hunted by ads and the commercialism that makes you want this and want that, whether you need it or not, that I don't go to the store anymore. I only go when I absolutely have to. I find that if I put things down on a shopping list, about half of them I erase a couple of days later, wondering why I even put them down! And I've gotten a detachment from things. I've given away a number of things that I had to others who could either use them or put them to a worthy cause. And I'm not as bothered now when I lose something as I was ten years ago;

so, that whole aspect just really affirmed to me the material thing.

2. Then there's the whole sexual revolution in our day, and I just found my own life was just being destroyed by sexual fantasies that would come up totally unexpectedly because they were imprinted through television or the movies of our day. I got away from television; I found that my mind, kind of, gradually was relieved of these things. It took several years but it did lessen and more peace came. I just found a whole, more wholesome, true way of life began to develop with a lot of peace. I was not hassled all the time with disturbing images that unfortunately got recorded in the past, but I try to keep away from them now.

3. The third key area that I find prevalent in our American culture that was affecting my life was (I'll use the old traditional word) PRIDE, or the American heresy — you're #1, have it your way.... All our advertising is focused on the glorification of the individual — and I just found that that whole aspect, too, began to soften in my own life so I'm much more, let's say, at peace. I find that I don't need to put myself forward as I found I was prompted to do in the past. If things work out, fine. If they don't, I find the Lord opens other doors, but that "pulling oneself up by your own bootstraps" mentality and "having it your way," is kind of sick in our society.[19]

"It is time we hear from our Church on the great danger of television. It is destroying our minds, our faith, our families, our children."

A letter from
Port Washington, New York

CHAPTER NINE

IF SAINTS ARE MADE SO BY THE CHURCH BECAUSE THEY LIVE THE SPIRIT OF TRUTH, ARE THEIR WORDS NOT ALSO TO BE ACCEPTED AS THE SPIRIT OF TRUTH?

What do the saints who lived before and during the era of television tell us?

Padre Pio was disturbed and disgusted by television. He realized it would destroy family life and told everyone not to buy one. Regarding cinema or one might say, "sin"ema, he always gave the same answer: *"The devil is in it."* Could it be that a man whom the world recognized as extremely holy, who heard countless souls in confession and would tell them sins omitted, could also have correct discernment about television?

What does television do to us? What will happen when we watch it? Amazingly, you can go back approximately 17 centuries to what St. Augustine wrote and which rings more strongly in truth today than it possibly did then. Saint Augustine (354–430 A.D.):

> *"The affection I had for shows and the theater had*
> *been the cause of my continual indulgence in sen-*
> *suality; and I always came away more unchaste*
> *than when I entered because what one sees or what*
> *one hears excites bad thoughts, seduces the mind,*
> *and corrupts the heart."* [20]

St. Cyprian (200–258 A.D.) states:

> *"Theaters are a school of impurity and a place*
> *where modesty is prostituted."* [21]

During the time of ancient Bishop Salvian of Marseilles of France:

> *"It was the custom at the Sacrament of Baptism to*
> *make an extra renunciation; namely, a promise to*
> *'avoid' going to theaters."* [22]

St. John Chrysostom's (347–407 A.D.) belief was:

> *"He wished that all would fly from theaters as*
> *from a plague."* [23]

Tertullian (Third Century), in his book, <u>Spectacles</u>, states:

> *"Christian religion has an extreme aversion to all sorts of public amusement and the Church abhors them and Christianity cannot, in any way, approve of them."* [24]

It's amazing. These ancient saints and Christians actually speak more clearly of today's media than anything said in the present time.

So many have the attitude: everybody has it, everybody watches it, how can it be that wrong? Nuns watch it! Priests watch it! This wide acceptance of this medium does not make it right nor does it reduce our accountability. We will have to answer to God for our sins which television can cause. Moral truth of five hundred years ago is the same today and while television has desensitized us to these things, we will still be held accountable. Hasn't Jesus told His followers: *"You've heard of the sin of adultery. I tell you whoever allows it in his heart, commits the sin."* Doesn't TV constantly put in front of us occasions to sin? A man is a fool to think he can sit in front of it and not be affected by it — whatever is on. In <u>Airwaves From Hell</u>, the priest/author states:

> *"Unfortunately, so many have succumbed to the 'everybody is doing it' mentality that it is hard to*

convince them that, yet, temptations of all kinds
are bombarding 'senses' through this medium, the
most popular, prevalent, and easily accessible
form of seriously sinful entertainment." [25]

American Saint Elizabeth Seton had a vision she couldn't understand in the middle 1800s:

"Every American would have a black box in their
home through which the devil would enter." [26]

This one statement by Saint Elizabeth, being who she is, a declared saint of the Church, should strike the heart as lightning in exposing the black box. Go to any outlet store and look at hundreds of those black boxes destined for the home and reflect on whether this American saint is wrong about the devil entering the home through it.

Pope Pius XII makes a prophetic and profound statement about television (in the days of Ozzie and Harriet) about the home that substantiates Saint Elizabeth Seton's prophecy. Pope Pius XII states:

"Everyone knows well that very often children can
avoid the transient of attack of a disease outside their
home, but cannot escape it when it lurks in the home

*itself. It is <u>wrong</u> to introduce risk in any form into
the sanctity of the home surroundings.* " [27]

We should be stunned by these words as well as Saint
Elizabeth Seton's; that we have become so desensitized that we
no longer see the eternal damaging danger in the sanctity of
home. <u>This is a pope speaking.</u> <u>It is a saint speaking.</u> Have
times changed? As you have already read, during Lent, 1996,
Pope John Paul II made headline news from his balcony in the
Vatican as he called for everyone to <u>turn off</u> their televisions for
Lent.[28] Almost no one listened because the world, and those
who are of it, prefer lies to truth.

A great orator of the Third Century, Lanetantius, writes:

*"I know not where you will find more corruption
and vice than in a theater. Beautiful language
causes sin to appear charming. Fine poetry and a
pleasing delivery seduces the mind and leads it as it
wills."* [29]

Father Jozo, parish priest at the beginning of the apparitions in Medjugorje, presently tells pilgrims repeatedly:

*"Get rid of your idols; destroy them through
prayer and fasting; replace the TV with an altar,
put the Bible on it; get rid of the mountains of*

newspapers and magazines, all the human words, and listen to God; give yourself time to read His words."

Again Fr. Jozo said on August 18, 1996:

"The television, especially commercials, is the most destructive thing that has ever come against man."[30]

Father Rene Laurentin, the renowned theologian who has presented much evidence to the Vatican regarding Medjugorje, states:

"Television: The same principle applies to the artificial desires created by our civilization: 'You should also abstain from television,' the Virgin advised, according to Jelena (the innerlocutionist from Medjugorje).

"This abstention can only be beneficial. It would give an opportunity for silence and openness to God. Anyone who is in love will find the time for love. If we love God we will find the time for prayer. We have to borrow the time from elsewhere. Why not take the time that is uselessly spent in the mediocre activity of cultivating the television set, an activity that helps us 'avoid silence,' and pa-

pers over the hidden sorrows and the anguish in
our hearts. God is the remedy, the way to over-
come it, the solution: not a stopgap solution, for
we who are made by God can find our fulfillment
only in him." [31]

What we listen to and to whom we give our ear is important. Even in Medjugorje, TV invaded with full force. Some women spend part of their day watching American soap operas. One woman, losing sight of reality, went to pay a stipend for a Mass at St. James Church so a soap-opera couple who broke up could get back together. It is important not only to protect the eye but also the ear. Who has ours? St. Francis De Sales spoke of giving importance to what or whom we incline our ears:

"From time immemorial, women have worn ear-
rings, particularly, no doubt, for the pleasure of
their tinkling. Scripture says that Isaac offered some
to the chaste Rebekah as a first pledge of his love.
This has a mystical meaning. The ear is the first
thing that a husband should take possession of in
his wife and that a wife must keep for her husband
alone. Nothing but the sweet music of chaste words
ought to enter it. Therefore, remember always that if
the body is poisoned through the mouth, the heart is
poisoned through the ear." [32]

How many wives give their ear, not to their husbands, but to empty words from daily talk shows' advice, soap operas, or those people who are influenced by them; all of which form them not toward their husbands but toward what they hear and see. The husband's ear tuned to the game on the box, in turn, tunes the wife out. He is not able, then, to take possession of her ear. It is dangerous to give the TV a center position in the family, even in a small way. If done, there will be a loss of peace and disruption in the family unit. The family is then destined to spin apart because the center has no grace to hold it together. The TV, being a "center" for the family, impacts and directs it as a shepherd leading sheep. However, the shepherd of the family is the father, not the TV; and he is ordained by God to lead it. This not only holds true for family life but also for religious communities. When a TV is put in their home or center, it is destined to fly apart because this medium, as a center, has no grace, cannot hold, and anarchy follows. In Father Al Winshman's interview, he was asked:

> **Question:** *Father, we get a lot of mail, and a lot of nuns have written us over the years. Many of them are from orders that are in deep trouble, disbanding, or breaking apart. Television is always mentioned somewhere in their letters. There's frequent watching of television in their orders and they are losing community life, a lot of it, because they are watching TV every night.*

Father: *Yes, there isn't community life. I haven't experienced a deep community life, myself, in years. I have to make it myself. I'm afraid we're losing it in the modern age with the priests and the nuns. They're not identified as such in public, and, unfortunately, many of them are hooked on these American ways. I can't go places with some of my own brothers at times, because I disapprove of the amusements in which they participate. And I say, "This isn't right," but they say, "Oh, it's not going to bother anyone."* [33]

Father Al Lauer, a diocesan priest of the Archdiocese of Cincinnati, in his booklet, "The Bible on Sex," says:

"Also, until we shut off or throw out the TV, we'll probably never be free from extreme sexual temptations. What used to be called pornography is now prime time TV. We can't expose ourselves to garbage without constantly smelling the stench. We can't watch TV without the constant smell of sexual temptation." [34]

*"Your latest book really opened my eyes. I quit
watching TV shows for Lent this year and never
went back. But now I understand that the real cul-
prit is the 'box' itself. So out go all the video tapes
and the box."*

> *A letter from
> Racine, Wisconsin*

CHAPTER TEN

THE TRUTH FROM THOSE IN
THE INDUSTRY ABOUT THE MEDIUM

We have mentioned Our Lady's messages, what the saints and priests have had to say, but what about TV's own promoters — people who helped build the industry? What do some of them think?

Marshall McLuhan, professor at the University of Toronto, known as **the high-priest-philosopher** of TV and quoted in almost every source where TV is concerned, from his books has made known the statement:

> *"The medium is the message" (medium meaning television).*

He says it's not so much the content which shapes people, but the medium itself. <u>**At this point in these writings this may be difficult to understand that the box, the television itself, shapes people.**</u> However, this astounding revelation will be made clearer to you once you've read further. The point now, however, is that bearing this in mind, the fact that the TV itself shapes

73

people, not necessarily what is shown, gives more evidence of its being the Piper's pipe to seduce man during this century. He also has observed that *the "mass **media** of today are turning the world into a 'global village,' shrinking the globe with respect to shared experiences and passing new ideals or experiences to every individual on earth."* [35] This, of course, fits perfectly the bad apple principle of satan's plan and the necessity for networking people together.

We are led to sin many times by temptations which are used by being brought up from stored memories, which many times have been put there, or stamped there, by what we've seen in order to lead us to sin during the present or future. Is this diabolical?

Ron Miller, National Syndicated TV critic says:

"As we enter an era of computerized technology that threatens to make TV an ever-more-passive part of our lives than it is now, it is frightful to imagine that somebody might be hatching some <u>diabolical new plan to manipulate our stored memories</u>." [36]

Martin Esslin who has had a life's career in TV states that in the future, 100 to 200 years from now, the greatest disaster of the 20th Century may well be "American television."

Irving Settel writes:

"One fact is clear: because of television's impact, the world will never be the same again. Our future has been set on a new course in every respect imaginable, in every social institution, custom, belief, or set of values."[37]

Are we to be pleased with television? By its own people, it is stated that it is changing every custom, belief and value! Statistics and breakups give evidence to what sort of change has happened.

Newton H. Minow, head of the Federal Communication Commission, which regulates TV, etc., spoke to the National Association of Broadcasters in Washington, saying:

"I invite you to sit down in front of your television set when your station goes on the air and stay there without a book, magazine, newspaper, profit and loss sheet, or rating book to distract you and keep your eyes glued to that set until the station signs off. I can assure you that you will observe a <u>vast wasteland</u>.

"You will see a procession of game shows, violence, audience participation shows, formula

comedies about totally unbelievable families,
blood and thunder, mayhem, violence, sadism,
murder, Western bad men, Western good men, pri-
vate eyes, gangsters, more violence — and car-
toons. And, endlessly, commercials — many
screaming, cajoling, and offending. And most of
all, boredom. True, you will see a few things you
will enjoy. But they will be very, very few. And if
you think I exaggerate, try it." [38]

The view he expressed probably would not surprise anyone; however, it is a shock to learn that Newton H. Minow said
the above in 1961! He was appointed by President Kennedy
and during that time the TV was like Disneyland compared to
now. His insight and truth about TV, as a vast wasteland, caused
him to be replaced. **This action (his being fired) in itself speaks
of the power the medium has in not ever being able to speak
against it.**

What about science? What does it tell us regarding television? The most frightful uncovering of what the TV *really* is,
fortunately, is now being exposed by scientists. After learning
about it, one is able to understand to a much deeper depth why
Our Lady says to **renounce and avoid it.**

"Thank you for the book on TV. It is all true and may thousands come to read this; believe it; and get rid of the box of misery!

"I have been telling my husband and children for twenty years most of what is in this book. Of course, no one was interested and our family paid the price with suffering brought on by the devil's medium."

> *A letter from*
> *St. Paul, Minnesota*

CHAPTER ELEVEN

THE UNCOVERING OF THE MEDIUM
WHAT DOES SCIENCE REVEAL?

Before television, communication took place in an orderly sequence of words; then through mental steps, plus recall of past experiences while listening or reading, you would come to a conclusion. It was logic. For example, an apple has a stem, it is semi-round, red, thin peeling on the outside, with seeds in its core. To listen to or read this statement, you go through mental steps. Your brain analyzes each step and puts together a mental picture from them, which you conclude from what you heard, and also from past experiences concerning apples that are already stored in your memory. You had to be alert, in a state of attentiveness. What science has found and proven is that television skips most of these steps in the brain and it is just there in image. Because the image of an event is infinitely closer to reality than any written or spoken account, television has a way of becoming more real than life itself.[39] Something happens that is different when you see a movie on television as opposed to reading the book. The book requires your effort, and when read, it is always better than the movie. Watching it on television you are passive, limiting your imagination to what you see. Understanding this is important to realize what the TV actually does to you when you watch it. The following paragraph, highlighted in bold print, is very important to grasp before going further and should be read several times until <u>fully</u> grasped. Before the following is read, it is important to pray, from the heart, to the Holy Spirit regarding what you are about to read about science and what TV does.

Researcher, Herbert Krugman, wanted to find out what happens to the brain of a person watching TV. Monitoring subjects' brain waves, he found repeatedly that within about 30 seconds the beta waves which indicate alert and conscious attention change to alpha waves which indicate lack of focus and lack of attention; the state of aimless fantasy and day-dreaming which is below the state of alert consciousness. When given something to read, beta waves reappeared. What surprised Krugman the most was how rapidly the alpha state emerged. Surprisingly, more research proved just as astounding: the left side of the brain is the side that accepted the step you just read about the description of the apple. It processes the information and critically analyzes it. The right side of the brain forms the images of what you think or see, receives information emotionally, and does not critically analyze it, leaving that job to the left side. The right side is where images are formed. It perceives the world in terms of moods, sensations, feelings, starts to form an image and is dependent on the left

side to analyze and logically help it to form the image. Krugman concluded, "the brain responds to the medium or television, not the content difference." In other words, the "medium," the "thing" causes the left side (beta) of the brain, which defends your thoughts, your values, to <u>tune out</u>, bypassing your logical reasoning process, going straight to the right side (alpha) which contains all the feelings and sensations to implant, prompt, stamp, or mark an image in your mind and which can be made use of in temptations. Krugman, along with other researchers, has found that watching television tends to shut down the left side,[40] thereby disengaging the information processing of this area of the brain. Krugman concluded:

> *"What you receive on TV is not thought about at the time you see it."*

If you were out in a park and a bad thought or image came upon you, as a Christian or just someone with moral values, you undoubtedly will try and cast it aside lest you sin. This is a temptation. To do this, you need both sides of your brain to process and analyze what the emotional side receives to conclude that this is wrong. If you keep the bad thought there and entertain it, you commit sin. The medium shuts down your alertness and full consciousness, processing information for you, which is presented in a ready-made image. The medium itself delivers the content directly to your mind, bypassing your protective guard of critical analysis and delivers you right into entertaining what you see because you are **not able to think at the time of exposure what it is you are entertaining.** Perhaps this is why Our Lady said:

May 25, 1987

"...You are ready to commit sin and to put your- selves in the hands of satan without reflecting..."

You cannot reflect because watching TV puts you in a position of readiness for sin, an occasion for sin. There is no ability to reason and reflect and defeat a temptation if it is already pre- sented to you and you entertained it. How many of us have seen scenes, bedroom scenes or lewd conduct, and watched for two minutes. If a temptation comes upon us with the same thoughts and if we don't immediately reject them, then we entertain the lewd thoughts. It is the Church and the Holy Scriptures which teach us that entertaining bad thoughts or images is sin. Just as Jesus said in the Scriptures, *"You have heard of the sin of adultery. I tell you, he who commits it in the heart has committed the sin."* If, therefore, it is a fact that the entertainment of adultery or any other lewd or evil action is a sin if committed in the heart why then wouldn't something which is more than a thought, which causes us to savor and entertain a lewd thought, not also be a sin? Soap operas, com- mercials, and a host of other shows contain a multitude of things that entertain the heart and thoughts that are in constant violation of God's precepts, holiness, and purity. Science proves we are below the threshold of consciousness when watching television. Can you use the excuse you didn't sin because you were not fully conscious, when you consciously put yourself in front of the TV, knowing from past experiences that it leads to sin?

Continuing the above message, Our Lady's next sentence (below) clearly relates that we have to be alert to choose God, protect ourselves, and not allow the television to put us in this state of unconsciously following satan because we have no ability to reflect because of the way the medium delivers us into evil.

May 25, 1987

> **"...You are ready to commit sin and to put yourselves in the hands of satan without reflecting. I call on each of you to <u>consciously</u> decide for God and against satan..."**

How can we claim to consciously decide for God if we place ourselves in a dangerous position in which a "medium" stops our ability to be fully conscious, and gives us no other possibility but to bring us to the occasion of sin and even to entertain sin at the medium's will? To watch it, we must ask ourselves, *"Are we deciding for satan?"* You cannot know what is coming or what thought or image will be thrown upon you in the next moment, and once you do know, you will have already entertained the lewd behavior which, if you continue, will lead you further into sin. But you do continue because what you have time to reflect on is what you've seen moments before not what you see in the present moment and that is if you stop at all because the medium does not allow you to reflect. It carries you immediately to other variations or scenes. So what you see has entered you and you anticipate the images coming up. This makes it impossible to protect yourself except to completely remove yourself from the TV.

Is it possible that the **angel of light, lucifer,** places just beneath our noses something so common to seduce us? This something is so common, yet reaches people of all walks, even those who cannot read. Settel writes:

> *"In contrast to the written word, television knows no illiterates. Tiny children understand what they view on the home screen, even cats and dogs seem fascinated. Communication via TV is both instantaneous and complete. **For the first time since Genesis**, man has the power to reach deep into the senses of all his fellows everywhere, with the <u>speed of light.</u>"* [41]

The way the television works is unlike any other "medium" which exists. It is a <u>deception</u> "<u>itself!</u>" We think it's the

84

content which comes across that informs us and even directs us; however, the medium, the television, the thing, the black box, whatever you call it actually does something to us. It is why McLuhan says:

"The medium is the message."

This is difficult to understand. How is it that the TV is the message, not necessarily the content? The following may help you to see it more clearly and should be read several times if not clear before reading the rest of the text until it is understood.

What you see on TV when you look at it is one small dot of light, less than the size of a pinhead.[42] **That's all, a single dot which is sent from its source, network, studio, etc. as an electrical impulse. If you could freeze the screen in a microsecond of time, the only visible thing would be this single dot. When it disappears, the next "single" dot appears — only one at a time. You remember where the last dot was and are watching the present dot and you are waiting and anticipating the next dot. No images are <u>ever</u>, <u>ever</u> there. You remember previous dots and hold them in the right side of your brain where the image is built and stamped in you. You <u>never</u>,**

never see an image; it is not sent through a wire or airwaves. It is made up in your very self, in your own mind, and all below your conscious aware-ness, all in a fraction of time. This medium dece-ives us and it, in itself, gets us to create in our-selves the images[43] it dictates. The television itself does this to us, actually putting the left side of our brain into semi-dormancy and sneaking in and stamping an image on the right side. This is why it is said that the "medium (television) is the mes-sage," it's not the contents. The television en-trances you and seduces you by its dictates and entertains the tendency to sin by actually forming the image, perhaps in somewhat the same way a temptation comes upon you, "except" the televi-sion continues to lead your thoughts which in turn will lead your heart. To subject yourself to this medium is very dangerous to not only the spiritual life but also to the soul itself. The content can be anything and satan has never had a problem find-ing bad apples to mix with good apples (religious or secular program content). The real message is the box. You fill in the motion and the picture. You are very involved, very busy, and all this activ-ity is only on one side of the brain; the left side is tuned out. This frees up the right side to accept

**and act upon suggestions, even commands. Simp-
ly put, you open your consciousness up to suggestions and even commands of the contents[44] which
is controlled and planted in you by the medium itself.**

Perhaps this is why in the beginning days of TV, thoughtful men were frightened by it because their spirits sensed what
their intelligence could not. Good, bad, religious, or secular
content does not matter, it is the medium itself that is dangerous.

Who controls this media/medium? Even McLuhan,
whom the TV Industry adopted as their high priest, after realizing how this medium works, **ended his career[45] because of the
research about the right and left side of the brain and the
process of the way dots, called electronic scanning, affect our
minds. Amazingly, McLuhan, the philosopher, the high priest
who helped build the TV industry, urged everyone to "pull the
plug" on television because he considered it deeply violent in its
effects on the mind and body!**

It is important to note that it is not the Community of
Caritas of Birmingham nor this author but the industry itself, or
people associated with it, who have discovered these things and
fully believe them. Christians would be ridiculed to suggest that
the TV is some kind of god. Yet, McLuhan recognized:

"Television is like the traditional concept of God whose "center" is everywhere and whose margins are nowhere. All seeing, omniscient, all pervasive, all-encompassing, television comforts us in our loneliness and is always there in our time of need, ministering and giving unceasingly, for free." [46]

Tony Schwartz, author of <u>Media</u> states: "Ask anyone raised in the religious traditions of the Western World to describe God and this would be the answer:

"God is all-knowing and all powerful. He is a spirit, not a body and He exists both outside us and within us. God is always with us because He is everywhere. We can never fully understand Him because He works in mysterious ways. In broad terms, this describes the God of our Fathers but it also describes the electronic medium, the second god." [47]

Could it be possible that perhaps Christians are the last to understand what many of the industry themselves believe? Is it possible that with the separation of the right and left side of the brain that the will of God would be clouded or too difficult to discern? To discern and know what is right requires rational, analytical thought and reason. One person shared that she sometimes thought she had a vocation but she had difficulty discerning. She completely stopped watching TV, listening to the radio, and using other media and she began to strongly sense a vocation and she finally heard the call and was sure. Does it not stand to reason that those "Divine commands" from God are clouded and interfered with when the left side of our brain is shut down or dulled into inactivity through television? At the point of no longer hearing God's commands, who's commands do we hear? Abstinence from this medium give us the ability to think more clearly and to discern more correctly.

"There was no doubt about it; my father was very much a family man. But there were two shows that he watched on TV that we did not dare to interrupt. We had to be silent."

A letter from
Springfield, Illinois

CHAPTER TWELVE

SOUNDS OF SILENCE

Writer, Joyce Nelson, states:

"We are in danger of collectively responding to the god-like promptings of media echoes in the right hemisphere (of the brain) as though they were our own volition (decision)." [48]

It seems that television has become a god over many people, even unsuspecting Christians; however, we should be the first to know and yet we understand little in comparison to secular sources.

Media advisor, Jerry Grafstien, said in March, 1983:

"Television is god." [49]

These people really believe that this is a god because it can suggest and command people in an "anti" way. God does this in our inner hearts through our reason by "divine promptings" (inspiration). In the year 40 BC, a pagan named Publius Verquil spoke of a divinely-born child to come who would bring peace to the world and a new age. He described this event as one centered on a smiling, infant son whose cradle was a cornucopia of flowers and whose birth would bring about freedom from fear for animals and mankind. Jesus fulfilled this prophecy. Many times in history souls, even pagans, have received prophetic understandings about different events in history. Music of the fifty's, sixty's, and later spoke prophetic truths of today. At the time they were written there was no understanding of what they now are revealing to us, as the following song shows:

THE SOUND OF SILENCE
(Simon and Garfunkel)

Hello darkness my old friend,
I've come to talk with you again.
Because a vision softly creeping,
Left its seed while I was sleeping,
And the vision that was planted in my brain
Still remains within the sound of silence.

In restless dreams I walked alone,
Narrow streets of cobblestone.
Beneath a halo of a street lamp,
I turned my collar to the cold and damp,
When my eyes were stabbed by the flash of a neon light,
It split the night and touched the sound of silence.

Sounds of Silence

And in the naked light I saw,
Ten thousand people maybe more.
People talking without speaking.
People hearing without listening.
People writing songs that voices never shared,
No one dared disturb the sound of silence.

Fools, said I, you do not know,
Silence like a cancer grows.
Hear my words that I might teach you.
Take my arms that I might reach you,
But my words like silent raindrops fell,
Echoed in a world of silence.

And the people bowed and prayed,
To the neon god they made,
And the sign flashed out its warning,
In the words that it was forming,
And the sign said the words of the prophets are written
on the subway walls and tenement halls,
whisper the sound of silence.

The darkness of TV has become a friend to many in their loneliness, softly creeping, placing images that form as a seed grows while one is in the daydream state of sleepiness — planting its vision in your brain all in the deception of silence. The TV's most active time is in the night, stabbing the eye by its neon light. It hides and soothes over the cold and damp feeling of loneliness with sound which is not human, rather manufactured. When exposed in naked light, multitudes talk yet do not really speak in the flesh; they seem to hear but do not. Thoughts you have or songs you hear while watching TV are never shared because the medium keeps you mesmerized. No one dares to <u>interrupt the sound of silence of those loved ones present in the room with you</u>, who themselves do not want to be talked to while being stabbed in the eye. Family and friends become fools sitting together in silence while sounds blare all around — a real sound of silence of no communication between loved ones. Silence like a cancer grows.

But Our Lady calls us, *"Hear my words that I might teach you; take my arms that I might reach you."* Alas She says, *"But my words like silent raindrops fell; echoed in a world of silence."* Our Lady's words cannot enter the home of a family "silenced" by the sounds of TV. But it is what the people want, for the people bowed and prayed to the neon god they made. AND the sign flashed out its warning, in its <u>own</u> words that it was forming. False prophets' words of filth that one finds on subway walls and building halls counter the words of Our Lady. *"The sign said the words of the prophets are written on the subway walls and tenement halls, whisper the sound of silence…,"* a sound so silent, it is deafening to all who hear it, killing the social exchange between one human and another.

Pause and reread now the words of the song. Its meaning will be clearer and more prophetic to you.

How can Our Lady penetrate the silence caused by so much sound? We must be willing to turn away from that which makes death seem life and life seem death. The remainder of this chapter will prove this point.

To use Our Lady's words, **another "uncovering of deception"** and another piece of evidence is that everything that has life has a presence, an aura, something that dead things don't have.[50] Evil desires to kill life and effectively does so with the television, not the contents but the very medium itself. The television eliminates "aura" and displays death as appealing! It conveys realistic images but cannot capture the aura of something living. Living things, the way God created them, become less when viewed through television.

Jerry Mander author of <u>Four Arguments for the Elimination of Television</u>, tells:

> "(Regarding his work) ... *with the Sierra Club to shoot images of the Redwood Forest in order to help them establish Redwood National Park. The footage he brought back just didn't work. It didn't capture at all the live redwoods and was flat and conveying nothing of the mood of actually being*

*there and the splendor. Mander decided to go
back and shoot again. This time, however, he shot
acres of dead redwood stumps. The images of the
stumps were more powerful than the living trees.*

*"Without aura, the image of a living being is life-
less, merely a detailed husk of an exterior surface.
The image may be entirely realistic, 'life-like,' indeed, but what it conveys is nothing more than
husk or shell. That means, he says, that communication through TV of dead imagery or non-alive
imagery is more efficient than communication of
living imagery. Since dead objects (advertised
products, a machine, or corpse) have no aura in
the first place, it loses nothing in the process of being translated into an image but the living thing
loses its most important quality which is life es-
sence…. So television (not the content) accom-
plishes something that in real life would be impossible, making products more alive than people."* [51]

This anti-human medium that makes a can of soup dance
across the table, gives something without life, life. Real life is
diminished, making it less than it actually is. This follows satan's
desire — death for mankind, nature, or all life on our planet.
Our Lady warns us and reveals his intent:

January 25, 1991

"...satan is strong and wishes not only to destroy human life but also nature and the planet on which you live..."

Our Lady clearly states satan's plans, his "desires." Is it coincidental that <u>television</u> does and promotes what the above message of Our Lady states? The present attraction by the world to spiritual death is obvious. It should be even more apparent that a real spiritual medium is spiritually directing it. Prophets of evil predicted plans to make the dead living. This is in line with satan's false promise, *"follow me and you'll live forever,"* which is always death. Before the turn of this century, a press report, November 29, 1881, stated:

> *"The ghost will walk (speaking of photography) and that's how, little by little, science, progressing with giant steps, will succeed in abolishing death, its sole obstacle and only enemy."* [52]

Another press quotation from the year 1875, speaks prophetically of the time coming of the life the medium will give us:

> *"When at last color photography has been achieved and when phonograph has been added to that, then movement and speech will be caught si-*

multaneously with vigorous accuracy, that is to say, life itself. When that day has come — and it's coming tomorrow — science will have given us the complete illusion of life. <u>*Why shouldn't it be capable of giving us life itself?*</u>" [53]

"After reading this book so many things made sense...for example: when I was a school teacher, there were students who were 'zombies' in my class. One boy in particular sat there with a glazed look. He told me he watched TV from the minute he got home until he went to bed at night....so sad for a third grader."

A letter from
Fort Collins, Colorado

CHAPTER THIRTEEN

THE EDUCATION MYTH

So science uncovers the evils of TV, but what of the uses of TV for good purposes? What of using television for educational purposes? A study of half a million sixth through twelfth graders in 1980 showed: the more TV, the lower the achievement, regardless of the number of hours spent doing homework and reading.[54] A prevalent philosophy is that TV works against the education of a child. The right/left brain phenomena is enough to tell us that in a daydream state one does not learn. There is a great deal of other research that supports that TV does not educate; and rather than teaching, it entertains and actually damages a teacher's ability to compete! Teaching vs. entertaining. While we will not go deeply into it, a good deal of research is easily available that TV does not educate; it entertains and in the long run harms one's ability to be educated.

In Joan Anderson Wilkins' book, Breaking the TV Habit, she writes:

> *"Have you ever really looked at a child in front of the tube? The poor thing looks like he's had the*

child knocked out of him. It is unnatural for a
child to be anything but active and busy." [55]

We at Caritas have seen in real life experiences what really happens when the TV and videos go out the door. Our
children suddenly had to be creative. Their boredom was
healthy because it fostered creativity. Suddenly joy and real
laughter were heard coming from their hearts rather than a
devious chuckle because of the TV. Their innocence is being
protected. They are being allowed to just be kids. They play.
Really play. We've seen for ourselves that TV, aside from its
other evils, diminishes children's ability to play and amuse
themselves. In May 1994, 25 **liberals**, physicians and psycholo-
gists in England, sent a shock wave through their whole country.
They signed a statement declaring that mistakes have been
made in not protecting children's innocence. Other liberals and
the media were outraged. It reads:

> *"Many of us hold our liberal ideals of freedom of*
> *expression dear, but now begin to feel that we were*
> *naive in our failure to predict the extent of damag-*
> *ing material and its all-too-free availability to*
> *children. By restricting such material from home*
> *viewing, society must take on a necessary respon-*
> *sibility in protecting children from this, as from*
> *other forms of child abuse."* [56]

Aside from the medium and its damage, what about supposedly "good" contents of kids' shows like Walt Disney's "The Lion King?" It is no secret that there has been a gravitation of individuals over the last decades who have influenced the television and movie industry. Many of them and their lifestyles contradict, in every way, Christian precepts. Their ideals, many perverse, show up infiltrating their productions, hidden or in the open. "Newsweek" reported that "The Lion King" is a "message" movie, telling us there is no need to fear strong women, and giving some wrong definitions about family and environment. One father said:

> *"To let my children see a movie, produced by people whose lives, they believe, are normal but Christianity teaches us are abominations, makes about as much sense as to let my children play with rattlesnakes. I do not want anyone, through this medium, influencing my children and defining what family, home, or the environment are, especially when they are trying to do it subtly."*

A gentleman who left the TV business, in response to a question about the type of people who work in the television industry, said:

> *"They are a special kind, typical business people living according to the laws of the jungle. If I can't*

get him, he'll get me! They are people filled with hatred, crooked, lying as naturally as they breathe, hypocrites, setting themselves up while setting you up, playing vicious games. The hardest thing for me was to hear the blasphemies, and words in vain." [57]

"A few years ago my husband and I separated and my two pre-teenage boys moved in with Dad, while the two youngest stayed with me. I was blessed with the grace of two broken TV sets and continued to live without the 'box' for three years. My two teenagers decided to move back home and in my eagerness and blindness to please them, I allowed a TV to enter our home once again. I found it more difficult to stop their viewing habits and began to lose control of the little ones as well. My third son began to do very poorly in school and also began to give me many problems at home, especially with obedience and respect. I realized then that the TV was in control of my family. Only this week after reading your letter was I given the strength to return the TV (along with a copy of the book) to their father.

"Life has already improved one hundred percent. The younger children are enjoying our family time together and soon all four children will be together to enjoy this Advent Season together. It is so much easier to focus on our prayer life and to live the messages of Christ."

*A letter from
Rockledge, Florida*

CHAPTER FOURTEEN

OK, I ACCEPT EVERYTHING STATED, I'LL ONLY WATCH RELIGIOUS BROADCASTING OR TAPES

What about religious programming? Benedict J. Groeschel, C.F.R., spiritual writer and Franciscan Friar of the Renewal states:

> *"If you are really growing in holiness, you wouldn't be watching TV. You'd be doing good works with the poor or praying right now. In a certain sense I'm being facetious but in another, I'm not." (He originally said this on a religious television program.) He adds:*

> *"After work, we spend a good deal of time in life being entertained. The fact is Our Lord said for every idle word that men shall utter, they shall render an account. It is probably equally true that for every idle word that men shall listen to they shall also render an account. So the good Christian is struggling to have his life so organized that*

everything he does is directed toward the will of God
and toward being a better Christian."[58]

Father Frank Poncelet goes much further and believes
the television, regardless of its programs, must be thrown out.
Regarding the issue of programming or **religious** broadcasts and
programming, he states, it is too little too late.

> *"At this late hour when satan firmly controls most*
> *TV sources, individuals' and well-intentioned*
> *groups' only recourse, virtually the only effective*
> *means remaining, is to attack the instrument." He*
> *states, "When a gunman is at your door, ready to*
> *kill your family, you don't address a letter to the as-*
> *sociation he stands for or to the maker of guns. In*
> *fact, you don't even attack him — you go directly*
> *for the instrument he is holding, the gun, in order to*
> *save your wife and children. The time for your*
> *good intention, or hope of changing those in control*
> *of the gunman's organization has obviously passed;*
> *your only recourse is to get the gun out of his*
> *hands."* [59]

To receive religious broadcasting, you have to receive
many other things which come with it and which at sometime or
another will be viewed. The book, Air Waves from Hell, addresses this argument very well, and it is recommended to be

read for further answers. **Sadly the biggest defenders** are sometimes those who justify keeping something bad because of elements of good within it. satan offers the shimmer of light, or truth, which he hates, in order to gain a foothold for his voice later. On a scale weighing good for the family versus bad for the family, good is far outweighed by the bad considering: family time, prayer time, communication with each other, and the buildup of sacredness in the family. The medium really offers none of these things with any measured success. In comparison, it promotes the ruin of family with bad behavior and the breakup of family.

If parents are watching religious broadcasting, are the children there with them? Most people say that their kids are off playing in another room, etc. Does this build family — or separation? Simply put, by its own virtues, Christian programming cannot do the things secular TV does to get and hold children's attention. Yes, maybe for a short time, but eventually you will find them wanting to turn to what the networks and cable offer. "Roger Rabbit" vs. "X." It was difficult to even think of a well-known religious, children's movie to make a comparison to show a point, so we made up one and called it — "The Moon and God." "Roger Rabbit" vs. "The Moon and God." Both of these are children's movies. "Roger Rabbit," even though a cartoon, breaks many, many Christian precepts which include seduction, bad language and appearance, smart-aleck behavior, disrespect and the presentation of vices in a cute, lovable, or favorable light. "The Moon and God" includes none of the above since it is Christian. Which will your children prefer to watch? Keeping the television for perceived good reasons, knowing it is a bad medium, is courting spiritual danger and disaster for yourselves and children.

Of course, the main point some use to justify television is the content of religious programming. Can the justification be used, bearing in mind the medium and what it does to you (brain phenomena, stamping images) which is already, in itself, enough reason to sufficiently convince you what to do? Regarding content, the medium itself, through deception, violates the free will whether it be good or bad content. For those who would argue a show is good, it's religious, how is it defended since the medium (television) not the content subverts the free will? Yes, willingly you place yourself in front of it, you do not have to do so, but once you do, the methods of the medium working in your brain have the ability to lead your thoughts, dominating you and not giving you time to think about what you are seeing at the time you are exposed to it. While it cannot be said that TV breaks the free will, its enslavement comes as close as you can get without doing so, and that in itself is dangerous and a violence to the free will God gave man. God, on the other hand, is not deceptive. You must consciously choose Him. Evil is there and good is there. He does not "snow" you to choose Him. He wants you to come to Him being aware of all the facts and in freedom. His is an invitation to follow. satan's is a command to follow. Our Lady said:

November 25, 1987

> **"...Dear children, you know that I love you immeasurably and that I desire each of you for myself but God has given to all a freedom which I lovingly respect and humbly submit to..."**

Our Lady's saying, *"I desire each of you for myself,"* is followed by "but," knowing satan desires us and will do anything — break all rules, seduce us to violate our will, and enslave us through vices, wasting time, etc. We knowingly and unknowingly give our free will to him through the medium. He will do whatever is necessary to take hold of us while Our Lady shows us that She stands before us humbly, quietly, with great respect and submission to man's freedom. **Justifying the viewing of television and keeping it because "I will only watch religious broadcasting" must be confronted and evaluated by the truths read.** Is it possible that God, who is truth, would want you to watch religious programming which is delivered to you through deception? By a medium which deceives? God cannot nor would not be for deception. He does not want to call us by deceptible means, but rather with our full consciousness and love to choose him. Jesus told the Pharisee, **"had I not come**

you would have not been responsible, but because you've heard me you are now accountable." Now that Our Lady has revealed truths to us about television deceptiveness, be it religious broadcasting or secular, we now carry upon us the great responsibility of knowing truth. If we choose deception, we may very well be choosing a path just as the Pharisees did, and by hearing Jesus' words, suddenly were held liable. We too can no longer claim to use a deception even for perceived good purposes such as religious broadcasting. Do not reject this point. It correlates with Scripture and Our Lady's words. Mirjana was told:

March 18, 1996

> "...**Accept My messages that you may be accepted**..."

Reading all the previous revelations, one now is confronted with making a decision toward good or evil. Our Lady tells us of satan's "active" plan to enslave man through "great" temptation and that this danger is through material (television, the first among things) and the world (contents on the television which presents us the world). Our Lady says:

June 25, 1989

"...Pray because you are in great temptation and danger because the world and material goods lead you into slavery. satan is active in this plan..."

Even if you already have (or haven't) made up your mind, another aspect is needed to put a complete picture together in order to see in real depth what has been placed in the world during this century. The Scriptures tell us to avoid silly and suggestive talk. It says we are not even <u>to listen</u> to it for our holiness forbids it. So how can one justify a medium in which children's cartoons contain such talk?

If this century does not belong to God, and Our Lady has told us there are evil things, and we consider the principles of the Pied Piper and networking the world together (the rotten apple) — what would the instrument be? What is it that Our Lady comes for twenty-nine years[*] to "uncover" and deliver us from? Sin, yes! She said to renounce sin. But what is the primary instrument this world offers which leads man to sin? Why is it She is with us to close out this century? What kind of hold does satan have on us that God sends Our Lady to the earth daily for over a decade? If indeed this century has been dominated by something other than God, then would not the

* Refer to footnote on page vii.

Book of Revelation have insights to reveal to us about these things? Would Revelation not relate to a time in history when the dragon is all powerful? Why would Revelation take place when he is much weaker? Our Lady says satan is strong!

January 14, 1985

> **"My dear children, <u>satan is strong</u>. He wishes with all his strength to destroy my plans. Pray only, and do not stop doing it. I will also pray to my Son so that all the plans that I have begun will be realized. Be patient and persevere in prayer. Do not permit satan to take away your courage. He works very hard in the world. Be on your guard."**

"I was overwhelmed by this book. After praying, then reading it, I couldn't believe I am so blind all these years to satan's deceptions.

"My father died at home in a hospital bed of cancer in 1976. As he lay in bed, the portable TV was to his left and a crucifix on the wall to his right. Although he was heavily sedated for pain the last few weeks, he was visibly distorted and agitated at the presence of the TV. My mom finally removed it from the room, and the last two days he had his eyes fixed on the Crucifix. Can't help but think how many hospital rooms filled with terminally ill persons are forced to face satan in their last trials unable to remove him or his channel."

A letter from
Ogema, Wisconsin

YOU'VE READ WHAT THE MESSAGES, SAINTS, SCIENCE, AND THE SECULAR SAY ABOUT THE MEDIUM; BUT WHAT ABOUT THE BIBLE?

Pope John Paul said in a homily:

"Mary (Rev. 12) carries the features of that woman whom the Apocalypse describes ... The woman, who stands at the end of the history of creation and salvation, corresponds evidently to the one about whom it is said in the first pages of the Bible that she 'is going to crush the head of the serpent.'" [60]

Mary is referred to in the beginning of Genesis, and presently, She is with us at the end of this time of man in the midst of this great struggle about which Apocalypse describes. In Medjugorje, Our Lady said:

August 2, 1981

> **"A great struggle is about to unfold, a struggle be-
> tween my Son and satan. Human souls are at
> stake."**

The Pope went on to say in his homily:

> *"She it is with whom the apocalyptic dragon makes
> war, for being the Mother of the redeemed, She is
> the image of the Church whom we likewise call
> Mother."* [61]

When we study Revelation, it becomes evident that Our Lady's
message parallels it. Her constant call to conversion is just what
Revelation encourages. A recent book about Revelation called
The Navarre Bible — Revelation, Text and Commentaries,
states:

> *"The Revelation of John constitutes a strong call to
> conversion. It urges people to commit themselves
> to God and put their trust in God."* [62]

Indeed, the Book of Revelation seems to collaborate
with many events taking place. It is not to say they won't also
apply sometime in the future, but Holy Scripture is living, not
dead. It is multi-purpose. A verse can speak to us now regard-

ing something, and ten years from now, it can also speak to us about something completely different.

June 25, 1991

> **"…If you pray, God will help you discover the true reason for my coming. Therefore, little children, pray and read the Sacred Scriptures so that through my coming you discover the message in Sacred Scripture for you…"**

This message was given on the tenth anniversary of Our Lady's appearances in Medjugorje. Why does Our Lady say, **"discover the true reason for my coming"** and **"read Sacred Scripture"** to know? Why do we not already know Her true reason for coming? Surely it would seem after ten years we would know. What is it after sixteen years (as of June 1997) and hundreds of messages we still are to discover — and in Sacred Scripture at that? Pope Pius XI speaks of self-indulgence, greed for possessions, and said:

> *"The disease of the modern age and the main source of the evils we all deplore is that "<u>lack of reflection</u>," that continuous and quite feverish pursuit of external things, that immoderate desire for wealth and pleasure, which gradually causes the heart to lose sight of its nobler ideals, drowning*

them in a sea of impermanent, earthly things, and preventing them from contemplating higher, eternal things." [63]

Does not television exactly represent the above?

Remarkably, Pope John Paul II said regarding the **beast** in Revelation, that aside from the interior struggles of the heart, in regard to rebellion in the modern era, it (the beast) will take on a concrete form as the **"content"** of culture and civilization as an ideal and philosophy or a program for action for the shaping of human behavior. The Pope says:

> *"It reaches its clearest expression in materialism, both in its theoretical form — as a system of thought — and in its practical form — as a method of interpreting and evaluating facts, and likewise as a programme of corresponding conduct."* [64]

The single "thing" which encompasses the Pope's statement in all areas of thought and the shaping of human behavior is TV. Our Lady's message of March 25, 1996 fits the above like a glove:

"...In this time, when due to the spirit of consumerism, one forgets what it means to love and to

cherish true values, I invite you again, little children, to put God in the first place in your life..."

Unfortunately TV is in the first place in families all over the world. It is in the first place in promoting behavior through consumerism — *"buy this; get this; desire; want; lust for; have; you deserve."* Most incredibly Our Lady says of **"consumerism"** that it is a **"spirit."** By what She says, we know this spirit is not of God. So these questions must be posed: "Where does this spirit dwell?" *"Where does its voice cry out the loudest?"* *"What does it make as its first throne?"*

But how could we be so deceived? St. Cyprian writes of satan:

> *"...because he moves silently and seems peaceable and comes by easy ways and is so astute and so deceptive that he tries to have night taken for day, poison taken for medicine. So by deception of this kind, he tries to destroy truth by cunning. That is why he passes himself off as an angel of light."* [65]

Perhaps then we should ask how could we not have been deceived? We quit praying. We accepted this "thing" without question. It stands to reason, a far superior and more advanced intellect could deceive us. satan is the master of deception. Who do we think we are, not praying and not living holy lives, and still expecting the intelligence and spiritual wisdom to see what the great deceiver has done? So now Our Lady comes to give us the wisdom, tell us how to obtain it and grow holy, and to reveal the evidence piece by piece. Now She leads us to Holy Scripture to learn the **"true reason for my coming."** So turning to Revelation in prayer, we began to understand. The following may seem simplistic because it is. Materialism and consumerism can be explained in volumes of complex ways; however, for common man, everything can be simplified as follows.

Revelation, Chapter 13, speaks of a beast and the "dragon" (representing satan) which gave "it" his own power and throne, together with great authority. satan gave this beast or "thing" his full authority to captivate the whole world, for Revelation 13 says:

"In wonderment the whole world would follow after the beast."

What fits this description? Revelation 13 also says:

"Then I saw a wild beast come out of the sea..."

The very first time airwaves were used, "a message" was broadcasted from a ship at sea to the shore.[66] The following is stated from a historical source:

122

"The proving ground of radio was the sea, the one part of the world which could not be reached by a wire." [67]

It can then be said that radio came out of the sea and radio through music, useless chatter, and many other things promoted the world — lewd behavior, lust, and want. We wake up to it, get out of the shower to it, get in the car with it, jog with it, eat with it, shop with it. We virtually cannot escape it — in public stores, bathrooms, restaurants, etc. What else before the radio has honored satan and promoted his interests as much? Its promotion of evil no one can stop. Revelation 13:4 says:

> *"Men worshiped the dragon for giving his authority to the beast; they also worshiped the beast and said, 'Who can compare with the beast, or come forward to fight against it?'"*

Through it, disrespect toward God and constant blasphemies against Him have come upon the earth twenty-four hours a day, non-stop. Verse 5 says:

> *"The beast was given a mouth for uttering proud boasts and blasphemies,..."*

Radio and the "medium" continue to boast about their greatness, and it seems to become more boisterous as each week, month, and year pass by, not only being content to commit blasphemies against God, but now anything and everything holy, including His saints. Verse 6 says:

"It began to hurl blasphemies against God, reviling Him and the members of His Heavenly household as well."

Has any instrument of man's history fit this description as this medium does today? And what part has it had in influencing Christians to accept many errors, to be plagued with many problems, and in dominating the way we and our children behave? Verse 7 says:

TV & radio

"The beast was allowed to wage war against God's people and conquer them. It was likewise granted authority over every race and people, "language" and nation."

God allowed Job to be tested. War was waged against him. Can we reasonably question whether permission was granted to try the world during this century? What kind of beast is there that could have authority over every **"language,"** let alone every "nation," "people," "race," and even enter into "God's people?" Could it be carried by airwaves to all the languages and nations? Reason and think! Isaiah says, *"Come reason with Me."* Reason, Holy Reason, based in God's word, precepts, and

124

Church teaching can help you see light? This is something God wants you to do, but if blocked by media, you are not able to reason toward truth. Your mind is influenced and occupied. The second beast, Verse 11–15 says:

> *"Then I saw another wild beast come out of the earth. It had two horns like a ram, and it spoke like a dragon. It used the authority of the first beast to promote its interests by making the world and all its inhabitants worship the first beast... It performed great prodigies; it could even make fire come down from Heaven to earth as men <u>looked on</u>. Because of the prodigies it was allowed to perform by authority of the first beast, "<u>it</u>" led astray the earth's inhabitants, telling them to make an idol.... The second wild beast was <u>THEN PERMITTED TO GIVE LIFE TO THE BEAST'S IMAGE</u> SO THAT THE "<u>IMAGE</u>" <u>HAD THE POWER OF SPEECH</u>...."*

TV's voice is transmitted through FM radio. TV's image gives life to the voice. Is there any thing or beast in history that could match this revelation so perfectly? Does John, a First Century man, describe, as best he could, man perhaps looking at TV with the screen making fire come from Heaven? Prodigy is defined as an extraordinarily marvelous or unusual accomplishment, deed or event. Man, when TV first came into use, was saying these things about this medium. In the book, <u>A Pictorial History of Television</u>, television is referred to as:

"Infant prodigy." [68]

It would be hard to understand how John would not be amazed at the vision he saw. All this is enough to make your skin crawl and cause disbelief, but the next verse is important also. Science has shown us that TV deceptively forces and stamps an image directly in the right side of our brain by bypassing our logical, analytical left side. Under normal reasoning conditions, the left side allows us to more easily understand God and His desires for us. The television, advertising, and associated industries universally accept the methods and end results of right/left brain phenomena and dot scanning. Tens of millions of dollars have been poured into research to better understand how to "prompt" people into buying products or ideals. President Carter, 30 points behind in the polls, hired and paid one of the leading experts in the world on these methods to build an advertising campaign to manipulate and prompt directly the image that he should be president. Everyone was surprised, some even shocked at how he swept into the presidency. About the only ones who were not surprised by it were those whom he hired to do just that. They knew their tactics work. There are one-hundred-million-dollar companies guided by people who understand these powerful methods and utilize them. These methods are used not only to sell products, but to buy any and everything, even political offices! More and more, everything bought or sold is beginning to come under the control of this unseen force. From the book, The Perfect Machine, is quoted:

"The techniques derived from knowledge of the right hemispheric (brain) processing (by the medium) and appeals is now standard procedure in political campaigns and public relations efforts."[69]

There is so much information which proves this that many books could be filled. It is not from the religious or extremists but from those in the industry itself, and it is this evidence which helps us see the following. **All people of the earth, all classes, are influenced through an unseen, yet intelligent, knowing, deceptive force. This force has the ability to imprint an image on the right side of the brain and influence people to submit to "false, divine" promptings. It leads multitudes, not only toward evil, but also to buy and sell everything from food to political offices.**

Continuing, Revelation 13:16–17:

"__It__ (beast) forced all men, small and great, rich and poor, slave and free, to accept a stamped image on their right hand or their forehead. Moreover, it did not allow a man to buy or sell

anything unless he was first marked with the name of the beast..."

An image placed in our mind that is deceptively forced upon us without our even being fully conscious of what this medium is doing could easily be described as a mark. Coupling all of this with Our Lady's message calling consumerism a spirit, breaks all doubts left in regard to the medium.

"THE DEVIL'S EYE" — 1979 rock song

Can you hear me, are you listening, has your programme disappeared?
I can see you, I am watching you, I've been planning this for years.
I have blacked out your television, every station in the world is mine,
And there are millions who are just like you as you sit there, paralyzed!
I have some orders which you will follow, and there's nothing you can do,
'Cos as you're looking at your TV screen, I am looking back at you...

> *Oh side by side,*
> *We will cross that Great Divide,*
> *'Cos nothing's gonna save you now from the Devil's Eye!*
> *Oh nothing's gonna save you now from the Devil's Eye...*

Turn your dial to the number that is shining on your screen,
You will notice that everything is red, you won't need blue or green,
All around me, fire is burning, yes I'm calling you from hell,
And all those people who haven't seen me yet, will soon be under my spell.
Something's happening, sounds like thunder, maybe the Lord is on His way,
He's still angry and He's after me, since I cheated on the Spanish train,
Oh yes He's coming, and He could stop me, but He'd better make it soon,
'Cos the last time that I won a world, I made it into a moon...

> *Oh side by side,*
> *We will cross that Great Divide,*
> *'Cos nothing's gonna save you now from the Devil's Eye!*
> *Oh side by side,*
> *Forever we will ride,*
> *'Cos nothing's gonna save you now from the Devil's Eye!*
> *I can see you,*
> *I can see you, I can see you...*

Sung by Chris Deborgh

CHAPTER SIXTEEN

IS THERE ANY DEFENSE LEFT FOR
YOU KEEPING THE TV?

How can it be? It's not reality! Perhaps Revelation just may actually be taking place. We pinch ourselves. How could it be we're alive while these verses may be coming into play? We almost can't believe it. We want to — we don't want to. It's supposed to be off in the future somewhere — yes, maybe around the corner. But not while we're alive. We are frightened by it and excited by it — all these thoughts at the same time. This writer feels the same way. It is almost unbelievable, but Our Lady's messages reveal it. The evidence keeps coming. It is there. But logically, what other time would it be, especially if satan has this century? The Scriptures say he will give his full authority to those beasts who will speak blasphemies day and night to every man of every class on earth. Spanning the time of man, does anything fit these verses so clearly? They meant little to man for 1900 years, because he had no way to understand them. If John actually saw a vision of the way TV works, the buying and selling of products and ideas, would not the spirit of what he saw reflect that which he wrote — man being forced and imaged on his right hand and, moreover, not being able to buy or sell without the mark? John says everyone who bought or sold was marked by this beast. He may have used the word "beast" because his mind had no understanding of mechanics and machines. Would anyone in the First Century describe this medium as a beast? It may have appeared to him as though it had life, and back then, only animals or man could perform actions on their own. So describing a "thing" as a beast would be understandable.

We do not dare say Revelation means exactly this or that. The Church must do that, and we submit to the Church and even defend Her right to do so. However, the Church offers little on these verses. If and when She does speak, it will possibly happen because of insight brought forth from belief or actions of many of Her members regarding a particular matter. Then the Church, through the Holy Spirit, will make a judgement and guide us. Our Lady's messages are bringing about these insights. Prophecy is not completely understood until it is fulfilled, then everything begins to become clear.

A saint, who was a nun in the late 1800s, saw herself in a vision wearing medals on her habit. She was plagued by this, did not understand, and was even sometimes troubled at its meaning. Five years later when she attended a function in which she was a participant, military officials honored her by pinning their honorary medals on her. Although her humility was embarrassed by their action, she now clearly understood the vision she had had years earlier. [70]

In Revelation, as in most prophecy for that matter, it is this way. It cannot really be understood fully until fulfilled. In the Revelation verses you just read, only a few lines were cited, and some of the ends of the verses were purposely left out. This was not done to deceive you, but so you wouldn't be distracted by that which is still not understood, because perhaps it is still in the future or not completely fulfilled. What was shown was for insight about the medium, its description, and its deception which Our Lady is uncovering. We tell you that there are things left out so you know what you are being presented, and to encourage your own judgement. For example, verse 5 said the beast was given a mouth for uttering proud boasts and blasphemies. That is what applied to what was being written. The other part of the verse which we did not include so you would not be distracted from the point being made was: *"…But the authority it received was to last only forty-two months."* This, like the nun's example, is not clear in light of present times, perhaps because it has not been fulfilled. In past history, early Christians ascribed this verse to Nero and his period of persecution. This proves that Scriptures have life, meaning the verse may apply to present and future ages.

Another example of a part of a verse being left out because it was unclear is: *"…the Beast suffered a mortal wound*

to the head..." One can only speculate at this point in the "present time" what this means, because nothing applies to the "mortal wound" unlike the case of the other verses which provided good, clear descriptions of the medium/media. As with the nun, it is not presently understood regarding the beast being mortally wounded in the head, "killed," yet somehow surviving. Although speculative, what is now presented is offered as an insight to what this could possibly mean.

Ivanka's apparition of June 25, 1989 took place in her living room. Those present gathered around the Crucifix which hung on her wall. Ivanka came in and prayed in preparation for Our Lady's coming. When the apparition occurred, one who was next to her observed her face closely, knowing that she was conversing with the Mother of God. He looked at her eyes and then at the wall to judge about where Our Lady was positioned, meditating on where Our Lady's eyes, Her veil, Her hands would be. Looking back to Ivanka, he felt great peace, knowing right there in front of him was the lap that Jesus sat on. He judged Her standing there, Her beauty, even though he could not see anything but a wall, but fully believing Who was before him and tracing where Her features probably were. He looked where Her feet would be, and his joy changed to a cold chill. He felt his skin crawl as though the Spirit of God came over him, for there where he judged Our Lady's feet would be was the top of the television set. The spirit of grace, giving his skin chills, spoke to him clearly — The Woman of Revelation crushing the head of the serpent!! Our Lady then gave the message we've already quoted during that apparition. It clearly can be applied first and foremost to the enslavement of TV and its offering of the world to us. The following message was given to Ivanka by Our Lady as She stood above and upon the black box on June 25, 1989:

> **"...Pray because you are in great temptation and danger because the world and material goods lead you into slavery. satan is active in this plan..."**

The mortal wound to the beast's head may well be Our Lady's coming for 29 years[*], Her coming to expose this beast through Her messages, the necessary weight to crush him. Her messages on the 25th of each month, which surely he must dread, are to go out to every race, class, language, and nation. They are to counter the opposite voice, the image, the **"medium is the message"** which also goes out to every race, class, language, and nation. In the last century and now this one, this medium has been successful in attempting every blasphemy by electronic wizardry. Our Lady is coming as the Woman of Revelation (Chapter 12) with a crown of twelve stars, clothed with the sun, to do battle with the dragon. Could it be that satan is coming through the beast, making prodigies of fire

[*] Refer to footnote on page vii.

come down from the sky on it, crowning himself with movie "stars" full of pride thus "anti-ing" Our Lady's stars? Is it his message that has prevailed over man and now Our Lady's message each month which must prevail?

The monthly message is given to Marija on the 25th of each month. Our Lady says these messages are "life" which flows once-a-month through sources. These sources are people, whom She Herself has chosen, who work worldwide spreading Her messages. The sources produce fruit as one would plant trees in different places on the Earth. Our Lady says this fruit, the "messages," which are crystal clear to Her children, are conveyed from the Throne of God. This is life-giving water being poured out as a river to the world through all the streets as medicine to heal the nations of the world. Our Lady produces the fruit to lead us to a time She calls "a new time," which means an end of the present time. In the end of the Book of Revelation, the last chapter of man, the end of the Bible, the very last sentences, read:

Revelation 22:1–2

> *"The angel then showed me the river of life-giving water, clear as crystal, which issued from the Throne of God and of the Lamb and flowed down the middle of the streets. On either side of the river grew the trees of life which produced*

fruit __12 times__ a year, __once each month,__ their leaves serve as medicine for the nations."

So clear are Our Lady's messages to those who accept them that Revelation comes to life for us. Though dormant for centuries, now Our Lady's messages, given **once each month** on the 25th, **twelve times a year,** will be the cure, **the medicine for the nations** of the world!

If Our Lady crushes this medium and what it entails through people turning against it and following her messages, will a future generation allow it to come back — survive this mortal wound to the head? We must ask ourselves what is so necessary that God sends us an intermediary daily for years, coming like an angel, if it were not for some great, historic moment for man. As the Israelites were led out of bondage, so, too, Our Lady comes to free us from the bondage of sin and those evil things which lead us to sin. The message from Our Lady which you read in the beginning of this book said:

April 4, 1985

> **"...I wish to give you messages as it has never been in history from the beginning of the world..."**

Could it be that we receive this grace from God through Our Lady because satan was allowed to **offer his message as <u>never before since the beginning of man, during this century?</u>**

All that you've read was presented to you **initially** from what Our Lady said, **secondly** from the saints, **thirdly** from secular media and the TV industry, **fourthly** from science, and **fifthly** from the Scriptures. Amazingly, these are five different sources quoted, ranging from Our Lady Herself, to scientists, Godless people, and even feminists, from various backgrounds and ideologies, that bring us to a point of decision. Perhaps it is why Our Lady continues to tell us to decide for God, because once we have understood, then there is a clear choice that must be made.

The most profound of all five groups, aside from Our Lady's messages, is that of science. It is not merely Christian belief or opinion, it is not just a few scientists who believe this medium, and not the content, is able to put an image on the right hemisphere of your brain and lead you subconsciously; but it is the whole media and industry itself. They speak of its power, and some are beginning to say it is a god. What is it, and what kind of hold does it have on us, that those who are not necessarily coming from a Christian prospective are saying, "<u>pull the plug</u>?"

Harvard theologian, Harvey Cox's view of mass media, is that **we should not try to use it, but try to dismantle it.**

As we stated with the detective and his example, when all the evidence is in, the picture becomes clear. From completely different sources, the pieces are put together, and we can now see why Our Lady said to **renounce television.** Could some of what is presented here be wrong? Yes, to some degree or another. But there is so much proof that the one who has given the authority to this medium has a hold over man, his direction in daily life, his actions and his role and behavior in society, that these writings are only the tip of the iceberg. What can we do? What are we to do? As the Book of Revelation states:

"Who can come against it?"

And also Revelation states:

"In wonderment, the whole world followed after the beast."

The following article, titled "The Lighter Side," was taken from the Detroit News, December 27, 1994:

> Hundreds of Bombay residents have tossed their televisions out their windows to protest violence and sex on Indian TV.
>
> It started a few months ago when Safira Alli Mohammad carried her family's set to the window of their high-rise apartment and threw it out.
>
> The tremendous crash caught the attention of nearby residents, and it soon began raining TV sets. All 1,200 families in area apartments now are reported to be TV-free.

CHAPTER SEVENTEEN

WHAT WE CAN'T DO AND CAN DO

What we can't do is react in fanaticism. <u>No one</u> should condemn another who has a TV once one decides to cast his out. Many are in a process of conversion and simply have not attained a level of spiritual understanding to grasp what this medium really does. The facts speak for themselves, and once one is presented with what is written here, he must be free to choose by his own free will that God has given him. Our Lady says:

1984 – 1985

> **"...It is necessary to respect the Commandments
> of God in following one's conscience..."**

A warning is necessary here because conscience and feelings are two different things. **Feelings can say yes, while conscience says no. A correct conscience must be based on God's precepts and His commandments. Then follow your conscience as Our Lady says. These writings appeal to your conscience, not to what you want or feel is correct.** Conscience, based on God's precepts, must dominate. Television by its nature appeals to your feelings. However, in the end, what one chooses to do is his right, by God's design, because He gave man intelligence and free will. God wants us to turn away from evil by choice, not force — by our love for Him. It would be fanatical for anyone to begin **demanding** others to throw away their TVs or condemn them for their use of it. Nor should you even condemn all use of it if some choose to use it. God will hold them accountable according to their knowledge. However, reading the preceding indicts those souls which have this knowledge. Being aware of its dangers, yet continuing to use television, places the soul into grave temptation and dangers. In other words, by reading these words, you are charged by the truth the words give.

What is stated is what Our Lady has shown us here at the Community of Caritas after years of prayer and discernment. It is quite clear where Our Lady has led us. The facts prove that anyone who has a desire for truth will come to the same conclusion. Truth has to come through invitation and enlightenment. It is Our Lady's way. Of course, parents have the right to make decisions regarding their children because they are charged with guiding them just as the father is with guiding the family. To impose on others outside of your immediate family or those you are not charged with guiding is not Our Lady's way. It has to be done through information and based on sound doctrine, appealing to man's conscience.

What we can do is pray that Our Lady will help us realize what She is asking of us. We can pray for change in our families, in the way we do things, and in the way we live in our homes. Although a major adjustment, many are now throwing away their televisions. The TV and the family, the holy family, the close family, simply will not go together. If Mary and Joseph would have had television available during their day, does anyone think that they would allow Jesus to see it? Those who for several years have tried to live what Our Lady asks are realizing more and more where She really is leading us. We are hearing from families who are realizing the destruction which surrounds this medium, such as the following:

Dear Caritas,   *9/20/94*

My husband and I are parents of two young children. We reached a decision concerning television that has had an impact far greater than we had hoped.

We were trying, as good parents, to limit the exposure our children had to unsuitable programs. Even though the programs we chose for our children were appropriate, the advertising of other programs that our children passively witnessed was very dark in spirit. It was our realization that it was humanly impossible to monitor 100% of the material viewed

*by our children. We realized that due to the content
of television, our children's gift of discernment was
being destroyed. They were being given a slanted
view of reality and family life.*

*Due to the removal of television from our home,
our family life has reached new heights. Our children's imaginations and physical play exceed our ex-
pectations. We interact on a deeper and more fulfilling level. We listen to music more often as a family.
We read together. We play games together. We
talk. We know each other more deeply.*

*Our children are our gifts from God. As parents,
we have been entrusted with them and asked by
God to lead them to holiness in life. Television interfered with our role as parents.*

*We now have more time to pray as a family, and
our life is becoming more and more fulfilling. It is
as if our vision has become crystal clear, and we
are able to experience, as well as do, God's will
more easily. It was not easy in the beginning to
turn away from television — yet, it was not as hard
as one would expect.*

Fairhope, Alabama

Our Lady called for the Year of the Family. Every obstacle in the family's way is to be removed if we are to experience joy and family happiness. "Things" do not help make families happy — love does. Two parents who love each other in their home will be such a delight, their children will forget the absence of television. This love will be like being under a warm blanket for the family, and everyone will want to snuggle under it.

"We read your book <u>I See Far</u>. After prayer and voicing our feelings/concerns, we as a family decided to give Our Lady a gift along with that of ourselves — our NEW $1200 TV and VCR! So as our consecration ended on December 8, we put a statue of the Blessed Mother on top of the TV, unplugged it, and said together three Hail Mary's. **As we were kneeling and praying in the living room, the TV <u>actually groaned</u>!** *We have a peace in our home that was felt immediately after turning <u>off</u> and <u>unplugging</u> 'the beast.'"*

A letter from
Lacome, New Hampshire

CHAPTER EIGHTEEN

EXORCISM?

Our Lady used two words in Her messages specifically concerning the television: **avoid** and **renounce**. To "avoid" as you've read means: to expel, to depart or withdraw from, leave, remove, to refuse to. To "renounce" as you've also read means: *"to give up by formal declaration."* These two words show that Our Lady is asking us to expel it and formally declare ourselves and our families, in prayer and action, against it.

One father did just that, realizing more and more the bad influence of TV. One night, after the family was asleep, he prayed the following over the television:

> *"Father, I see no fruit coming from this thing and as Jesus saw no fruit from the fig tree and cursed it and it withered, I, too, curse this 'thing.'"*

He did this knowing to remove it at this time would cause a war in the family. *Two weeks later, lightening struck it, completely frying the insides, destroying it!*

Exorcism?

Prayer is where the family needs to begin in removing the television. No one should expect lightning, as was the case with the father who prayed, but you can expect God to hear your prayers. Once you are able to expel it, you will have fulfilled Our Lady's request of renouncing, thereby avoiding it in the family.

A father, with his children, brought their TV to the Field at Caritas, where Our Lady had appeared to Marija in America, and they destroyed it. Then, in prayer, he consecrated his family to Our Lady and by this act, turned against everything that television offered. This was the renouncing he felt Our Lady asked for — a formal declaration. Since that first television was destroyed on the edge of the field, other families have come and destroyed their TVs, VCRs, and Nintendo machines and games also. When the families leave their TV's behind, they leave, filling the void by being attached and consecrated to Our Lady. Most of these families, feeling as they do about the medium, realize it would be a contradiction to sell it because doing so may cause someone else to fall because of it. They have chosen to set an example to their children and let them participate in formally destroying it as a family. It is a real lesson for them, and their family life becomes richer as the previous letter has related.

Exorcism?

Getting rid of the television may not always be so easy. To avoid and renounce the TV may be compared with the following three examples:

1. A cyst can be removed in a simple, one-day, out-patient surgery.

2. A tumor on the brain, which is serious and life threatening, may be surgically removed with patience and determination. After planning, prayer, proper order of medical steps, and necessary procedures, healing can possibly take place.

3. A tumor on the brain stem which cannot be removed and to do so would kill the patient. Living with it will eventually cause the body's malfunction and possible death but the only hope is for a miracle through prayer.

The first example is a couple who both see the light or who, through the husband's guidance and the wife's agreement, even if she doesn't understand, decide to destroy its presence in the family. Another example is a single person who decides to remove it. It's a simple procedure with few complications. Children will adjust easily if parents are unified in their resolve.

Exorcism?

The second is a couple whose husband wants to take it out but the wife opposes him. Even though he has the right to do so, the damage caused by his just throwing it away would be like a surgeon carelessly rushing into an operation to remove the tumor without proper x-rays and planning. He must proceed with gentleness and prayer for a month, year or even two, but eventually surgery must take place and when all other means are exhausted, the husband has the right to throw it out, even over the objection of his wife.

The third is the husband who refuses to remove it while the wife sees all the dangers. She cannot throw it out the way the husband above can, because by divine order, she has to accept the structure which God set up for the family. Hers is one of suffering and her only recourse is prayer, answered by a miracle. To badger, intimidate, and fuss would only be counterproductive just as would a surgeon's operating on an inoperable tumor. However, with a sweet disposition and fervent prayer, God will hear the wife and change the husband's heart through grace and her holy actions. Yes, it may take months or years but holiness is blessed with God's answer.

Youth or teenagers will react differently according to the parents. Parents have every right to decide what goes on in the home. A family is not a democracy and children do not run a household. Parents have no difficulty enforcing the requirement that their children go to school or brush their teeth. Two unified parents will quickly mute rebellion. However, a divided response of one parent who has the resolve while the other does not, will foster and continue the rebellion. Unity is your key to success.

These three examples are important because the attachment to television is so strong that it is actually causing families to tear apart. Family division, in itself, is a sign of a demonic hold, but as with an **exorcism**, one may experience reactions from family members which will shock you. Casting out the television has caused reactions in families no different than an exorcisms on demonics. Why would it not be the case with its holding power and strength over individuals of the family. A warning of great prudence, coupled with prayer, is vital and each situation must be evaluated. Once the television is removed, you can expect things in your life to be very different, but not abnormal. For sixty centuries and more man has occupied his time without television and that is the norm. The last 45 years with TV is abnormal compared to man's history. Joan Anderson Wilkins, in her book, Breaking the TV Habit, writes:

"Staying unplugged is not deprivation. In fact, many families report that after their decision to live without television, they feel free for the first time from the dictatorial hold television had had on their lives." She goes on, "After several years of talking to and counseling on how to turn off the

*TV sets, I decided to go to the children themselves
and began presenting **'No-TV Week.'** programs.
The children participated in these programs. The
children are enthusiastic and learn a great deal
about the medium they once took for granted. In
many cases, their parents are less excited."* [71]

When it comes down to it, children really don't want or
need TV. It is the parents who teach them the habit. Children
want their parents.

"Kids should run in the woods, swing from trees, swim in the creek down the road, and play 'hide and seek' half the night with the other kids in the neighborhood. My nieces and nephews sit in front of the tube with a mesmerized look that clearly shows they are below consciousness, and the images zing right into their brain with no critical thought whatsoever. One has to practically shake them out of a stupor to get them to come and eat. My brothers and sisters will not hear the words nor open their eyes to see."

A letter from
Davison, Michigan

CHAPTER NINETEEN

ARE YOU USING THE MEDIUM TO BABYSIT?

Parents who use the television to baby-sit their children, putting them bodily in front of it to quiet them down, do a great deal of damage to them. The camera is an eye and through this medium it will watch your children for you, making them quiet and docile. This is a very tempting thing for a parent who wants a little quiet. But parents who do this are the losers and years down the road these decisions will produce bad fruit. Granted, there are many who do this in ignorance, but selfishness is usually the motivation. *"I'll turn the TV on so I can do my own thing or work."*

Mirjana, the visionary, said of Mary, while living upon the earth, *"Mary always put Herself second. She never, ever once put Her needs first."* Evidence tells us that watching TV damages children's creativity and their ability to play. They get a distorted view of reality. There is research for this.

We, at Caritas, have experienced this ourselves. Once when the adults and parents of the community were meeting, the children played for over an hour, "cutting up," imagining, noisily — but really playing with joy. They've learned to do this since we gave up TV. In our meeting, we were discussing the ills of television when we decided to conduct an experiment. One office had a TV to review tapes sent to us and all the adults gathered in that large office. One went out to tell the children simply, *"We have a movie on TV for you to watch."* They came more quickly than if we had called them to supper. We suspected what would happen but it still amazed us. Within two minutes, all the laughter was gone, all the joy had left. Their faces became serious, drone-like with no happiness shining through. Cheerful smiles gone, they sat as if under a witch's spell — and this was a religious movie! Yes, there may be a laugh every now and then, but it's not the same laugh of joy from the heart. It was strong proof for us that what the TV philosopher, Marshall McLuhan, said was true: *"'the medium (television) is the message' not its contents."* Regardless of what movie we might have shown them, the resulting damage to their childhood — their capability of healthy play, social exchange, family exchange — would have been the same.

Joan Anderson Wilkins writes of the outcome in a neighborhood where a school's "No-TV Week" was implemented:

> *"The street was full of kids, everyone doing some-*
> *thing. The bikes were out, wagons were carting*
> *junk, basketballs were bouncing, nerf-football*
> *catching was going on the front lawn, it was like a*

three-ring circus. Neighborhood children needed one another more when television was out of the picture. It was apparent that 'No-TV Week' brought the kids together both in spirit and physically. It brought the community out of the closet and into each others' homes." She adds, "The children set up little retreats (hide-a-ways) in every corner of the house. There wasn't a blanket or sheet in the linen closet. Once inside their little retreats, the children read, talked, played with their Legos and Matchboxes and had fun. One other interesting note, the kids didn't gravitate to games. They gravitated to each other and their parents." [72]

She went on and wrote about the children picking up the hobby of reading and reading to each other.

Here is an important Bible verse to remember from Isaiah 1:18:

"Come reason with me, says the Lord."

Reason it out. What has civilized man done every night for sixty centuries? That's almost two and one half million nights. There must have been a lot of sitting around the fire. One father relates:

"I feel a fire is important to give us an incentive to gather together. I purposely turn the heat down and crank up the fire in the fireplace and then we bring out the blankets and gather around the fireplace. It brings us closer together as family, centered around the parents, instead of the TV, and we share a feeling of security. We talk and listen and sometimes just look at the fire, but we are warmed more by the love that is fostered by these actions than by the fire. Looking into the fire, we sometimes talk of all those who have gone before us, 1,000 – 2,000 years ago, and how those children sat around the fire with their fathers and mothers. Stories are told, life's lessons are taught, questions are answered. It is also a joy to let my children work with me in cutting and gathering the wood. A great deal can be learned from it. It teaches preparation, the value of work, and all this effort comes back to me in children who are balanced and directed by me rather than by someone in Hollywood.

"I see the TV as a real, living, thief, stealing memories and joys while implanting its ideals. To keep it there is to keep a burglar in the house. Families should take the money they spend on tapes and

*TVs, VCRs, and entertainment and save up and in-
stall a fireplace — not a cheap one, a good one —
big enough to produce heat and take up a wall,
with room for gathering around it. We all fall asleep around ours. It's difficult to carry my little
ones to bed every night when exhausted. It is a lot
more effort on me as a father because when coming home I cannot pursue my own interests. My
children, having no TV, want my attention. It is a
sacrifice of love and many times a decision must be
made against my own desires. But this is what real
fatherhood is about. However, by committing to it
our life, our memories, and our future will be richer for it."*

When you reason, you realize that the medium really
damages you and your family. By getting rid of it, you are freed
from its slavery and dictation to you, and the possibility of
really being a family begins to emerge. A father relates:

*"My wife and I began to go to charity outlets and
places which sold goods which were donated to
them for their cause and through them I purchased
some "National Geographic" magazines and began searching for more. I was able to put together
a semi-complete set from 1927 until now. I, in
turn, did the same thing with "Reader's Digest." I*

*built a library in our home, now having no TV,
and I read to my children. I have a good reference
source to bring to many of life's situations through
these and other books while my children are still
under my guidance. They really enjoyed this. It is
active, not passive like TV, when I'm there but not
with them in thought. TV brings me somewhere
else and we are all like isolated islands, bunched
together, independent of each other, with the waves
and winds of TV eroding our shore away, decreas-
ing our size, and making our family more separated. Reading brings us together. It's interrupted
sometimes with questions and doesn't always go
perfectly, but for the whole, everyone listens and
participates."*

Life without television will blossom, but only if you fill it with
something else: doing chores, participating in hobbies, walking,
reading, praying. In fact, it is dangerous to rid yourself of the
TV, sweeping your house clean, getting rid of vice and not filling
in the empty space. Being cleansed is not enough because there
is a great desire by evil to dirty what God has made clean and in
order to bring about a fall, a host of evil will come upon what
has been cleaned. Filling the emptiness is crucial. Jesus says:

Luke 11:24–26:

> *"When an unclean spirit goes out of a man, it roams through arid wastes searching for a resting place; failing to find one, it says 'I will go back to where I came from.' It then returns, to find the house swept and tidied. Next it goes out and returns with seven other spirits far worse than itself who enter in and dwell there. The result is that the last state of the man is worse than the first."*

The following letter shows how one family protected themselves from future attack and filled in their empty space that the TV left.

Dear Caritas of Birmingham,   *10/12/1994*

"For the past 15 years, our family has not watched television. This began because of our circumstances living outside the U.S.A. But, living without TV soon became a habit, and then a firm choice. Our seventh child is due in December and we feel thrilled and blessed that our kids know how to spend their time and their God-given talents. We do not mean to brag, so much as to share that it is possible and fruitful to say NO to television. Our

161

kids read incessantly, play musical instruments, sew, bake, create stitchery projects, compose poetry and act. They can problem-solve, take on immense responsibilities, reach out to help others, and defend the truth. We firmly believe they are adept at many "real-life" things, because they are not dependant upon living life vicariously in front of entertainment machines. And — most importantly, they have NOT been bombarded by the constant materialism, commercialism and erosion of values which is sadly a steady TV diet of America and the world.

"Many of Our Lady's messages have attested to the evils of television and have beckoned us to rediscover the simple, precious value of being together, appreciating each other, and cherishing the presence of Christ in each family member.

"The hardest part is the initial decision. Yes, you will be different. Yes, you will be judged and even ridiculed and, yes, my husband does miss watching sports. But, instead, he's been able to work towards a Master's Degree and has taught himself the beautiful art of stained glass. Yes, there is sacrifice but the resulting gifts, blessings and discoveries are incomparable.

"I like to imagine if all of Catholic America alone would fast from television, what a shock-wave of awareness we could send to the entertainment industry — a potentially profound message: 'We've had enough. We do not need your emptiness and perversion. We dare to be different. We will choose to spend the time in loving one another as Our Lady, Queen of Peace, invites us to!'"

In the Hope,
Love and Promise
of Jesus and Mary,
An American Family in Argentina

A while back, a professor from Russia visited us here in the Community of Caritas and we gathered together for a community dinner. She came in and the kids were playing in their typical way. It was loud and they were being very active. We told her to excuse the noise. She responded:

"Noise! This is life. TV is noise."

A profound statement and her insight about TV was just as interesting. When asked what the greatest threat to Russia was she said:

163

Are You Using the Medium to Babysit?

*"Television! TV is a total waste of time, destroying
creativity and destroying the youth in Russia. It
leads to destruction of respect, honor, and values. It
is sadly sweeping through Russia, leading youth into
all kinds of fads that lack purpose and wisdom. Yet
the youth imitate and follow it. Since TV entered
our homes a short time ago, crime has drastically
increased, divorce, which was unheard of among
those who are Christians, is rapidly increasing, and
families are breaking up. We survived Communism
but we won't the TV."*

Indeed, a great deal has been lost by man in exchange
for the deceptive value of television and this is becoming more
and more obvious. It's not just "Christian weirdoes," as the
worldly might tend to say, who think it's demonic or horrible.
Feminist author, Adrienne Rich, says:

*"Television 'itself' breeds passivity, docility, and
flickering concentration."* Her perspective is:

*"... The television screen has throughout the world
replaced oral poetry, old wives tales; children's sto-
ry-acting, games, and verbal lore; lullabies, playing
the sevens; political arguments, the reading of
books too difficult for the reader, yet somehow
read; tales of 'when I was your age,' told by par-*

ents and grandparents to children, linking them to their own past; singing in parts, memorization of poetry; the oral transmitter of skills and remedies; reading aloud; recitation; both community and solitude. People grow up who not only don't know how to read, a late-acquired skill among the world's majority; they don't know how to talk, to tell stories, to sing, to listen and remember, to argue, to pierce an opponent's argument, to use metaphors and imagery and inspired exaggeration in speech; people are growing up in the slack flicker of a pale light (TV) which lacks the concentrated burn of a candle flame or oil wick or the bulb of a goose-neck desk lamp; a pale, wavering, oblong shimmer, emitting incessant <u>noise</u>, which is to real knowledge or discourse what the manic or weepy protestations of a drunk are to responsible speech." [73]

In addition to this, Joyce Nelson, in her book, writes:

"Obviously, making TV programming 'better' does not rectify all the losses listed by Adrienne Rich, <u>each</u> of which has to do with having the left hemisphere of one's neo-cortex (brain) effectively amputated by TV, while the right hemisphere is colonized" (taken over by the medium). [74]

It is interesting to note that those voices whose ideology one would expect to be most opposed to Our Lady's request to renounce TV are the most in tune, as opposed to Mary's children, who one would think would be most willing to justify its destruction. Many of Mary's children knowingly keep it, not only in the face of Her messages, but also in spite of the brain-damaging effects of TV, along with its capability to have one in or on the brink of sin before one knows it, as well as an unlimited list of other reasons.

The Cover

The cover of this book, "*I See Far*," shows the domination the black box has over our being as well as our mind. The illustration shows the eyes completely blocked by video tape, its contents delivered by the medium directly into the mind, thereby completely dominating and confusing (rather fooling) it. It becomes one with the mind demonstrated by the mechanism resembling the brain. The light, which cannot be seen by the individual, shimmers off his face, hands, and scissors. He struggles in torment while he is torn between holding onto darkness (television) which he supports with his right hand or severing the tape. The black box (TV) which keeps him in bondage can be easily removed from his eyes by simply cutting it with the scissors he holds in his left hand. Simply cutting it will allow him to see the light and be free, for his mind to be elevated toward things of God. Sadly the cover speaks the truth, that it is by one hand that we support this vile box, knowing at the same time deep down inside of us that we hold a simple solution in our other hand. The question that confronts and convicts us after reading the truths about this mind dominating slavery is clear. Which decision will you make — the hand severing it or the hand supporting it?

CHAPTER TWENTY

A REVOLUTION TO BEGIN!

It is hoped and prayed that these writings begin the start of a revolt among not only Christians, but all people to throw this medium away, destroy it — not sell it. We invite anyone who wishes to consecrate themselves and their family and formally accept the invitation of Our Lady to make the decision to remove this medium from their home and consecrate their families and time to Christ through Our Lady's plans. Ask Our Lady to intercede to Her Son to correct all errors and take away all the accumulated garbage in you and your family because of this medium by your formal act of turning away. It is also hoped that hundreds of organizations will spring up to teach and show people these dangers. If you go and tell anyone **"the TV is the voice of satan,"** you will damage your case. Has your opinion about the TV changed after reading this? If anyone tried to expose to you in one paragraph, in a short conversation, about all the above, a typical response would be, *"He's weird."* Don't make that mistake. Give them this book instead, and pray. To do otherwise will birth a movement against those who are now ready, through Our Lady's invitation, to abandon and reject the medium You would also become people who, *"you are not to take seriously."* However, presenting all the evidence, such as you have here, proves itself and truth will prevail in all hearts who are open. It <u>will</u> show them if they want truth. Prudence and a lot of wisdom are necessary not to close the mind of people who are dominated by this medium. The evidence is all there if they are open to seeking answers. You will not have to worry about persuasion.

The intent of these writings is to light the spark through Our Lady's messages to alert people to the anti-message. It won't be done by us or different associations, but through prayer. Then through collaboration with Our Lady we will meet success. We must live what Our Lady asks.

When we hire a baby-sitter to watch our children, that's exactly what the baby-sitter does, sits and watches them, takes care of them. It is frightening that what is referred to by the TV, does the same thing as the sitter. It sits there as the TV "set," watching them. Scripture states:

Ezekiel 20:5–7

> *"...Throw away, each of you, the detestable things that have held your eyes; do not defile yourselves..."*

Jesus said in Matthew 18:19

*"If your eye is your downfall, gouge it out and
cast it from you."*

The time of realization has come, a time in which we
realize we will not clean up this medium and, even if we could,
what would it avail us? We can go on with hundreds of reasons
to get rid of something which has done more damage to the
spirit of man than any instrument in man's history on earth. It
inflamed the L.A. riots. It was the key element in beginning the
war in former Yugoslavia by showing each side, escalating in
horror, what the other side did until things erupted in full-
fledged war. It was the primary source to spread the idea of
plane hijacking. It fosters copycats. Think how many copycats
sprang from the idea of one person who put poison in Tylenol.
We forget that so many began to do this that the industry,
world-wide, had to begin sealing everything from Aspirin to
Nestles Chocolate Milk Mix. All because of the spread of a
warped idea through the medium. Television tends to make you
think and do what it shows you. Does not the family resemble
that which is now seen on soap operas, dramas, and weekly
comedy shows? The family has become the copycat and it no
longer represents something holy. Our Lady knows that we are
led and inspired by what we expose ourselves to and Her plan
itself is based on witnessing. Through witnessing and living holy
lives it will spread to others who copy the witnessing and they,

in turn, will be copied. To call this copycatting does not seem appropriate so we say to imitate that witness or as Our Lady said on June 5, 1986:

"Dear children, today I am calling on you to decide whether or not you wish to live the messages which I am giving you. I wish you to be active in living and spreading the messages. Especially, dear children, I wish that you all be the reflection of Jesus, which will enlighten this unfaithful world walking in darkness. I wish all of you to be the light for everyone and that you give witness in the light. Dear children, you are not called to the darkness, but you are called to the light. Therefore, live the light with your own life. Thank you for having responded to my call."

Jesus is "The Witness." He is "The One" we should <u>copy</u> and all voices which lead us to do anything but that, we should avoid. And finally, the television is viewed as good, like an "angel of light," but in his new book, <u>Air Waves from Hell</u>, Father Frank Poncelet says:

"...THERE WILL BE NO REAL PEACE IN OUR CHURCH UNTIL THE 'INSTRUMENT OF EVIL' IS REMOVED FROM A SUFFICIENT NUMBER OF CATHOLIC HOMES —

SUFFICIENT NUMBER BY GOD'S COUNT, NOT OURS. ATTACK, DESTROY, GET RID OF THAT INSTRUMENT OF SATAN, 'TELE-VISION.'" [75]

Our Lady is now sent as an angel to give testimony to truth. Finally, in the end of the Book of Revelation, in the epilogue, Chapter 22:12–16, Jesus says:

"Remember, I am coming soon! I bring with Me the reward that will be given to each man as his conduct deserves. I am the Alpha and the Omega, the First and the Last, the Beginning and the End! Happy are they who wash their robes so as to have free access to the tree of life and enter the city through its gates! Outside are the dogs and sorcerers, the fornicators and murderers, the idol-worshipers and all who love falsehood. It is I, Jesus, who have sent My angel to give you this testimony about the churches. I am the Root and Offspring of David, the Morning Star shining bright."

Just as these writings were completed, the following monthly message was received from Medjugorje. Our Lady said:

October 25, 1994[*]

> **"Dear children, I am with you and I rejoice today because the Most High has granted me to be with you and to teach you and to guide you on the path of perfection. Little children, I wish you to be a beautiful bouquet of flowers which I wish to present to God for the day of All Saints. I invite you to open yourselves and to live, taking the saints as an example. Mother Church has chosen them, that they may be an impulse for your daily life. Thank you for having responded to my call."**

This message is beautiful and to have the gift of being presented to God as a bouquet of flowers is a cause of great joy. But this message is not one of sugar even though on the surface some may be tempted to view it that way. Television's example offers a path of ease, fun, entertainment and frills; it increases the craving for information. All the saints were examples of persevering in the face of great struggle, loving in the midst of difficulty, enduring prolonged sufferings and hardships, and crying many tears. Their joys were of a divine nature as opposed to those associated with earthly "things" and what they offer.

---

[*] The newsletter was finished on this date but revised and made into a book, March, 1997.

Turning away from the assumed pleasure of TV may be difficult but Our Lady's above message is asking for you to be a "<u>saint</u>."

THE END

LINGERING QUESTIONS, COMMENTS, AND THE ANSWERS

Dear Caritas,   *May 6, 1995*

"Although we agree with you on network television being mostly satanic, we feel that the Virgin Mary would not condemn television completely. There are so many great programs and videos that can be seen on television, ie: EWTN, The Trinity Network, and videos like <u>The Miracle of Fatima</u>, <u>The Song of Bernadette</u>, etc. We are able to say the Rosary with wonderful Priests, sitting in front of our TV. The Catholic Mass is also available on at least two channels daily more than once a day.

"People who throw their TV's out, are throwing the baby out with the bath water. They need a little self control. All sets have on/off buttons and they don't have to watch the trash programs. I am sure that Mother Angelica of EWTN would not suggest people throw out their sets. She probably would suggest a little personal discipline."

                                            Sincerely,
                                            Pulaski, Tennessee

Dear Pulaski,

"Thank you for your letter. We do appreciate your concerns and see your sincerity in what you wrote. In response, we do not edit Our Lady's words. What Our Lady says, we fully believe. She said to **'avoid television.'** *It is obvious Our Lady meant television as a complete whole because Her next words validate that She meant good programming by singling out the bad as separate. Her words go on to say* **'particularly evil programs.'** *This message breaks down TV — those programs which are not evil and those which are evil. It is clear Our Lady is speaking of both, putting particular emphasis on evil programs. Her words* **'avoid television, particularly evil programs'** *speak clearly that both sides of the spectrum are to be avoided. We have seen tremendous fruit in families who have followed Our Lady's words without compromise, and they are the greatest testimonies as to the truth we printed. We know many use T.V. with good intentions, and we condemn no one who does. We, ourselves, also did the same in promoting Medjugorje until Our Lady slowly revealed, through Her messages and the Holy Spirit, where She was leading us here in the Caritas Community.*

178

"You wrote that you are in agreement that TV is mostly satanic and also question the throwing away of the TV set as equaling to the baby/bath water analogy. It is important to note that satan always packages things this way, presenting some good, which he hates, in order to be successful in bringing much bad, which to be successful, he knows he must do. So people who bring in cable for these good intentions also bring in the sewer of many other programs and channels. Overall letters to us reveal that the on and off buttons are not always used. Human weakness prevails and children, as well as adults, view things they never should, not to mention the wasted time better spent in prayer, works of charity, reading, or being with family.

"In response to Mass and prayers on TV, one person wrote to us of a friend who has become a couch Christian, praying with the TV and even believing that by viewing Mass, they are attending it. We do not know of any theological judgements made that say you can attend Mass through the TV, and we find it difficult to believe, with the messages of Our Lady of Medjugorje, that She would bless these actions. She pushes and nudges us con-

stantly to make the effort, go to Mass, pray, etc. such as the following:

> **'Thanks to all of you who have come here** *(to Church),* **so numerous during this year, in spite of snow, ice and bad weather, to pray to Jesus. Continue, hold on in your suffering. You know well that when a friend asks you for something, you give it to him. It is thus with Jesus. When you pray without ceasing, and you come in spite of your tiredness, He will give you all that you ask from Him. For that, pray.'**
> *(December 1, 1983)*

The next day Our Lady said, regarding the cold:

> **'Be kind to come to Mass without looking for an excuse. Show me that you have a generous heart.'** *(December 2, 1983)*

Again on February 15, 1984:

> **'...When it is cold, you come to church; you want to offer everything to God. I am, then, with you...'**

And more confirmation that Our Lady wishes for us to go to a Church and attend Mass rather than watching it:

'My children, I wish that the Holy Mass be for you the gift of the day. Attend it, wish for it to begin. Jesus gives Himself to you during the Mass. Thus, look forward to that moment when you are cleansed. Pray very much so that the Holy Spirit will renew your parish. If people attend Mass with lukewarmness, they will <u>return</u> to <u>their homes</u> cold, and with an empty heart.'
(March 30, 1984)

"These are but a few of many messages that have taught us what Our Lady desires. We have also seen wheelchair victims go to church for Holy Mass, some who are daily communicants, so an excuse about Mass-watching for most disabled can be overcome with any who will to do so and attend. In the end, time spent watching Mass can be spent, with a little more effort, actually attending it. Our book on TV was through a very broad perspective which came through Our Lady's messages, of which we arrived through years of prayer. It is where Our Lady has led us.

181

"It is important to note the Israelites insisted on divorce. Jesus said their stubbornness is why Moses allowed divorce, which in the law of the chosen was accepted. Jesus upheld what truly God wanted and said no more divorce. Our Lady does the same in regard to TV. In our stubbornness, we at Caritas used TV in the beginning, falsely believing that it was so valuable in the rebirth of the Church when, in fact, the birth of the Church had not this media and yet grew with the most difficult of circumstances. We simply don't need it to spread Our Lady's plans and Christianity any more than the early Christians needed it.

*"We cannot speak for anyone else in regard to what they might suggest, but when it comes to suggestions, we will go with the Queen of Peace, and She suggests and invites us to **avoid it.** We found that difficult to do with it sitting in our homes, and it eventually led us to throw it out. We found peace, freedom, and joy in doing so, and we encourage and invite others to do the same, but condemn no one who chooses not to.*

"We hope this may give you a little more perspective, and we suggest to reread I See Far. It is of a

*nature and depth of which must be read several
times with deep prayer."*

A Friend of Medjugorje

* * * * * * * * * * *

Dear Friend of Medjugorje,

"What about the news?"

Pensacola, Florida

The following was sent recently by a pilot. It proves that
you don't get the truth, not only from the news, but even the
weather.

> *"The following is a conversation between myself, a
> pilot, and the Gainesville, FL flight service station
> on July 11, 1996, the same day that hurricane **Ber-
> tha** was predicted to hit the coast of Florida. The
> TV weather reports were painting a grim picture for
> Jacksonville by late that afternoon. It was blared
> across the TV screens on all the channels. Interstate
> 95 was already jammed by people who were eva-
> cuating. The text was as follows:*

GFS: *Gainesville Flight Service*
P: *Pilot*

GFS: *Good Morning.*

P: *Hi. N2285S is at Craig, and I want to leave later this afternoon northwest toward Columbus, GA and was wondering what time I could get out.*

GFS: *Whenever you want.*

P: *What about Bertha? I heard it was moving to the coast of Jacksonville by tonight sometime.*

GFS: *Who said that?*

P: *The TV shows it moving toward the coast, and people are evacuating several areas. The army guard at Craig has put all the choppers in hangars, and the FBO is taking my plane off tie-down and putting it in a hangar.*

GFS: *Well, I don't know what radar they are looking at, but I show Bertha two hundred miles east of Bermuda and not doing anything. She has sustained winds of one hundred three but is only moving at thirteen knots per hour. As a matter of fact, it was on a heading of three hundred ten degrees but has now turned to three hundred twenty-five degrees. The Carolinas may have a problem in a day or so.*

P: *So nothing tonight?*

GFS: *From what I can see, you can go have a nice dinner, take in a movie, and then leave.*

P: *OK, thanks.*

GFS: *Talk to you later.*

"I left that same night after sunset. At the time of departure, skies were clear and winds calm. Being a pilot, I have seen this more than once. With weather radar now accessible to virtually everyone, even to their homes, how is it that big TV stations can be so inaccurate in forecasting, which routinely goes way beyond in reference to time (hours in this case) in regard to radical changes in weather? I have only one conclusion — money and ratings. They thrive by people tuning in, and ratings bring more advertising dollars. Stores are hit in the panic buying, and the circle perpetuates itself. Add to that the moral decline as a result, and the next situation becomes more distorted, more exaggerated. Those nice smiles on TV are deceptive, to say it nicely."

* * * * * * * * * * * *

When Marija came to America in 1988 and spent two and a half months near Birmingham, she had daily apparitions from Our Lady. Many significant things happened and many messages were given. Two things were significant which shed

185

some light — not the words of Our Lady, but Her actions. When Our Lady appeared in the Field on November 24, 1988, before the apparition began, Marija said to pray and not take pictures. During the apparition, a TV team moved right into the middle of everyone near Marija. Our Lady gave Marija an important message for everyone, blessed everyone, and quickly left. There was joy over what Our Lady said and did but disappointment that She left so abruptly. We understood it was because of the intrusion of the camera, and from that point on, there was particular effort to ban TV crews from the Field.

As Marija's visit drew to a close, television stations exerted so much pressure that they were granted permission to set up their cameras early in the afternoon in the bedroom where Marija received Our Lady's apparitions and messages. Marija was out buying a few things in preparation for her return to Europe two days later. Everyone waited, and Marija was late. When she arrived, she said Our Lady had already appeared to her. She herself indicated she did not know why Our Lady went ahead and appeared rather than wait a few more minutes until she returned. Meanwhile, thousands had gathered and were waiting for Marija. Marija told them Our Lady still blessed them and prayed over them all. When Marija walked past the bedroom, she saw the cameras. She then nodded towards the bedroom and said, *"That is why Our Lady didn't wait, She doesn't care for that."* Quickly, we realized it was a mistake to

have allowed the television station to come in; and this was a
strong lesson.

* * * * * * * * * * * *

5/9/95

Dear Friends of Our Mother Mary
and Her Son Jesus,

"I am Bro. Tony Droll, originally from the small
town of Carey, Ohio. I had the privilege of com-
ing to Zambia as a missionary early in 1965 and
have since been involved in teaching, social minis-
try, refugee relief ministry and for the past 11 years
in pre-novitiate formation of young men who wish
to become Franciscan.

"For quite some time now I have been privileged to
be receiving your Caritas newsletter,* which I
prayerfully read and pass on to others. I have
found the words written in the newsletters to be,
without a doubt, inspired and the fruit of hours of
prayer. It is therefore one of my objectives to let
you know that I not only receive the newsletter and
read it prayerfully, but I deeply appreciate the fact

---

* I See Far originally was published in newsletter form.

that you send it. I work to spread the inspired writings of the newsletters.

"I recently read I See Far. I read it prayerfully over a period of a couple of weeks. I can powerfully relate to what you have to share. The scourge of television has been in Zambia for most of the 31 years that I have been here. It is small yet, with poor equipment. Even today, the single channel begins its programs at 5 PM and ends shortly before midnight. It has news, agricultural programs, household programs and a number of interviewing programs, local plays, time for the president to address the people etc. More recently they began to bring in some of America's trash such as Dallas, Dynasty, Bold and Beautiful, etc. which have absolutely no value whatsoever except to show the corruption in the lives of people. It is now moving toward films with violence and sexuality. For many years, President Kaunda banned absolutely any kissing scene on the TV (even mother kissing her son) and even that has changed. I can honestly say that I see the change in the lives and attitudes of our beautiful Zambian people when TV comes into their lives, especially with the children.

"St. Joseph's Mission, where I live at our Formation House, is in the rural area. In fact my entire ministry has been in the rural area, beginning with the very deep West of Zambia, 350 miles from a tar road or railway. In all my time here, I have never ceased to be fascinated with the way the African child lives and plays. I can attempt to explain it but only to see it is to experience it. They have NO toys or gadgets to play with and yet there seems to be no end to their brilliance in inventing new games. They play soccer from an earliest age with two stones for a goal and plastic bags wrapped tightly in a ball and tied with strips of old rubber from worn out bicycle tubes for their ball. They have running games and tagging games and every sort which stretches the imagination of the spoiled Westerner. They enjoy themselves so much that they shriek with laughter and joy. In fact they can be so noisy playing, with natural delight, just outside my room window that I often have to close the window in order to concentrate on my writing or reading. Why are they so natural and delightful? I believe it is because they have not been spoiled by the Western world and media.

"I come back to the USA for a home leave every three years (I would love to stop by Caritas some-

*time for a visit) and honestly enjoy sharing with my
family and friends. One thing I do not look forward
to, though, in the USA, and I do not find to be a joy,
are the American children. I am constantly shocked
by the way they sass and answer back to their parents, always demanding. They have absolutely everything at their disposal and yet demand more. They
have 50 times more junk and toys than they need,
and want more. They use whining techniques to get
what they want, and unfortunately, all too often, they
get it, which encourages them to use the same means
again. They eat so much junk food and sweets that
many of them are already out of shape before their
teens. In comparison to how I see a good percentage
of the American children, our little African children
are 'angels.' They are pure delight to be around.
Unspoiled. Creative. Bright. Intelligent. High spi-
rited. They can come to Mass, which can easily last
2 to 2½ hours or more and they do not make noise
or draw attention to themselves or make demands.
If in any way you can relate to my view of American
children, you would go absolutely flips over our
children here, beginning with the big eyed, curly
headed babies who ride on their mother's back unless they are sucking her breasts and who rarely cry.
Surely it must be all of the security from the natural*

contact with their mother's body that begin them on the path of being the delightful, undemanding little beings that they are.

"*I must watch myself; I could write on and on about the natural beauty and spontaneity of our children. And I would credit very much of this purity to the fact that they have <u>no TV</u>; compared to our <u>American children who are literal 'slaves' of the TV</u>. Last year in August I had the rare privilege of going into the very center of the Kalahari Desert with my Provincial, and good friend, from America. I am sending a photocopy of the article as it appeared in the local newspaper of my little hometown in Ohio. Take notice of what I have highlighted about the children. I think I have found one of the last places in the world where the purity of the children is of such beauty that it even surpasses that of our local children. Why? The answer, as it appears to me, is in the last paragraph where I am saying much the same as you wrote but considerably more brief and in different words.*

"*In conclusion, let me assure you that I fully support you and your ministry of bringing the Good News of Jesus through His Mother to as many people as possible. On my part I will continue to promote the same message here in Zambia as much as I am able."*

Bro. Tony Droll

The following is the newspaper article that Bro. Tony mentioned in his letter. It appeared in his local hometown paper in Ohio and it is about his experiences during his visit to the very center of the Kalahari Desert.

Brother Tony visits country "where the Lord dwells."

I recently had the privilege of making a journey deep into the Kalahari Desert, a trip which an American friend (priest) and I planned nine or ten years ago and only now were able to realize. It became more than a trip or a break from the daily grind of training young Zambians to become brothers and priests; it became a pilgrimage to where the Lord dwells. It was a prayer; a meeting with God, where there are few signs of life and fewer distractions to divert one from His presence.

The desert can be aptly explained by quoting the back of a postcard we found in Botswana, *"The Kalahari, the largest unbroken mantel of sand in the world is one of the least traveled regions on earth. It has its heart in Botswana but spills over into neighboring countries. Kalahari! The name brings to mind thoughts of unending thirst; land with white-thorned acacia shrubs silhouetted against a blood red sunset; of hunter-gatherers with poison arrows and loin cloths in pursuit of strange animals adapted to survive harsh conditions; of lions standing proud in the morning sun; of searing heat-hazed summers and icy winds howling over grassy plains. It is all of this and much more. It is one of the last places which remain larger than man's achievements, where the soul can soar untrammeled by signs of human development and where a journey can take on the dimensions of a pilgrimage."*

Considering the mystery to me of how they find water for their survival, there was an amazing abundance of animals to be found in the desert. Water or moisture must be present some place, but certainly not found by humans such as ourselves. We had to carry 100 liters of water with us, not just for drinking or the radiator, but also for the coffee, cooking (potatoes, onions, and beans), cleaning the single cooking pot and two cups, brushing our teeth, but not for shaving. When I arrived back home I had acquired a beard, so I kept it as a reminder of life in the desert, which was a prayer.

During our time in the desert we slept in sleeping bags on the sand (would you believe how hot it can be during the day and yet how cold it can be at night?) and woke with the first light of day or the sound of animals. We celebrated the mass, with missal, host, and cup, there on the sand, with animals close around. The presence of the Lord was evident and experienced. In the morning, before the intense heat, we walked for a couple of hours, in separate directions, until the bright red 4x4 land cruiser (which we borrowed) was barely in view. And just BE. No word needed to be uttered, from the mind or the lips; the heart itself spoke, and the ears of the soul could hear the reply of God, *"Do you believe that I am here and that I love you?"*

In the very heart of the desert we came across a settlement of the Bushmen. At first we saw their huts which are simply made of grass in a beehive shape. Inside, as we saw later, their cover against the cold of the night was the skins of animals. They came old and young, running to the land cruiser in greeting and curiosity. There was no option but the art of communication — without language. Having spent much time with the children of our deaf school helped in speaking with the hands and using expressions. Their language was particularly colorful with the clicks with complimented their gestures and expressions.

The children were particularly delightful in their simple purity, innocence, and beauty of character. To pick up these little children, I felt I was holding a gem more precious than all the diamonds of Botswana. To gaze into their eyes was like looking into a clear pure brook before it runs into polluted rivers and becomes part of the pollution; before it has a chance to become tainted in any way. To experience these children was a prayer in itself.

When allowing the sanctity of the moment to be blurred by the thought of the vast corruption in our modern world and <u>the deterioration perpetrated by the decadent values which are constantly before people's eyes in the Western media,</u> it gave me cause to wonder who are the real privileged people in our world; who are the most content and happy with themselves and their society; who are most in touch with and at peace with self and nature and God. It made me wonder what it really means to be civilized. Is our concept of development really a step forward or is it regression in regard to the authentic values of life and love. The brief meeting with the simple Bushmen provided much food for thought, more to reflect on and even more to pray about.

Would that we could be plucked out of the contaminated waters of the so-called progressive society and be returned to the brookwater purity and simplicity that once was, but has long since been polluted <u>by so much of what is being placed before our eyes.</u>

Endnotes

1. Tan Books and Publishers, Inc., *St. Michael and the Angels,* Rockford, IL, 1983, p. 84.
2. G. & C. Merriam Co., *Webster's New Collegiate Dictionary.*
3. Ibid.
4. "Paul Harvey News Program."
5. Father Frank Poncelet, *Air Waves From Hell,* The Newman Press, Long Prairie, MN, 1991, p. 84.
6. Confidential, private interview with Caritas of Birmingham.
7. Robert Mayniham, *A Model for Renewal,* 30 Days, Sept.–Oct. 1990, pp. 58–59.
8. G. & C. Merriam Co., *Webster's New Collegiate Dictionary.*
9. Irving Settel, *A Pictorial History of Television,* Second Enlarged Edition, Frederick Ungar Publishing Co., NY, 1983, p. 19.
10. Ibid., p. 15.
11. Ibid., p. 19.
12. Ibid., p. vii.
13. Ibid., p. viii.
14. "Paul Harvey News Program."
15 Irving Settel, *A Pictorial History of Television,* Second Enlarged Edition, Frederick Ungar Publishing Co., NY, 1983, p. vii.
16. Ibid., pp. xi–xii.
17 Relayed by Fr. Al Winshman in his interview with Caritas of Birmingham.
18. Irving Settel, *Pictorial History of Television,* Second Enlarged Edition, Frederick Ungar Publishing Co., NY, 1983, p. ix.
19. Interview with Fr. Al Winshman by Caritas of Birmingham.

20. Murphy & McCarthy, *Half an Hour With the Servants of God,* NY, 1889, Chapter XCIII.
21. Ibid., Chapter XCIII.
22. Ibid., Chapter XCIII.
23. Ibid., Chapter XCIII.
24. Ibid., Chapter XCIII.
25. Father Frank Poncelet, *Airwaves From Hell,* The Newman Press, Long Prairie, MN, 1991, p. 93.
26. Ibid., p. 93.
27. Pope Pius XII Encyclical, *Miranda Prorus,* pg. 226–227
28. Associated Press, Monday, March 11, 1996.
29. Murphy & McCarthy, *Half an Hour With the Servants of God,* NY, 1889, Chapter XCIII.
30. Talk given by Fr. Jozo to group of pilgrims on August 18, 1996 at Siroki Brijeg.
31. Fr. Rene Laurentin and Dr. Henri Joyeaux, *Scientific and Medical Studies on the Apparitions at Medjugorje,* Veritas Publications, 1987, p. 91.
32. St. Francis De Sales, *Introduction to the Devout Life,* TAN Publishers, 1990, p. 259.
33. Interview with Fr. Al Winshman by Caritas of Birmingham.
34. Fr. Albert Lauer, *The Bible on Sex,* Presentation Ministries, Cincinnati, OH, 1987, p. 17.
35. Les Brown, *Les Brown's Encyclopedia of Television,* Third Ed., Visible Ink Press, Detroit, MI, 1992, p. 349.
36. Ibid., pp. xi.
37. Irving Settel, *A Pictorial History of Television,* Second Enlarged Ed., Frederick Ungar Publishing Co., NY, 1983, p. viii.
38. Ibid., pp. 148–149.
39. Ibid., pp. viii.
40. Joyce Nelson, *The Perfect Machine - Television and the*

Bomb, New Society Publishers, Phila., PA, 1992, pp. 69–80.

41. Irving Settel, *A Pictorial History of Television,* Second Enlarged Edition, Frederick Ungar Publishing Co., NY, 1983, p. ix.

42. Joyce Nelson, *The Perfect Machine — Television and the Bomb,* New Society Publishers, Phila., PA, 1992, p 71.

43. Ibid., pp. 72–73.

44. Ibid., p. 72.

45. Ibid., p. 145.

46. Ibid., p. 95.

47. Ibid., p. 95.

48. Ibid., p. 80.

49. Ibid., p. 80.

50. Ibid., p. 146.

51. Ibid., p. 146.

52. Ibid., p. 151.

53. Ibid., p. 151.

54. Martin Esslin, *The Age of Television,* Copyright ©1982 by Martin Esslin. Used with permission of W. H. Freeman and Co., San Francisco, CA, p. 80.

55. Joan Anderson Wilkins, *Breaking the TV Habit,* reprinted with permission of Scribner, an imprint of Simon & Schuster, copyright ©1982 Joan Anderson Wilkins, p. 154.

56. Irving Kristol, *Less TV, Less Crime?* published in Focus on the Family Citizen, Oct. 17, 1994, p. 24.

57. Father Frank Poncelet, *Air Waves From Hell,* The Newman Press, Long Prairie, MN, 1991, p. 51.

58. Taped interview with Fr. Benedict J. Groeschel by Caritas of Birmingham.

59. Father Frank Poncelet, *Air Waves From Hell,* The Newman Press, Long Prairie, MN, 1991, p. 55.

60. James Gavigan, Brian McCarthy, Thomas McGovern, *The Navarre Bible — Revelation — Text and Commentaries,* using the Revised Standard Version and New Vulgage with a commentary by members of the Faculty of Theology of the University of Navarre, 1993, pp. 26–27.

61. Ibid., pp. 26–27.

62. Ibid., p. 18.

63. Ibid., pp. 128–129.

64. Ibid., p. 104.

65. Ibid., p. 98.

66. Irving Settel, *A Pictorial History of Television,* Second Enlarged Edition, Frederick Ungar Publishing Co. NY, 1983, p. vii.

67. Ibid., p. 20.

68. Ibid., p. 47.

69. Joyce Nelson, *The Perfect Machine — Television and the Bomb,* New Society Publishers, Phila., PA, 1992, p. 80.

70. A story relayed by theologian Fr. Rene Laurentin, in France.

71. Joan Anderson Wilkins, *Breaking the TV Habit,* reprinted with permission of Scribner, an imprint of Simon & Schuster, copyright ©1982 Joan Anderson Wilkins, p. 152.

72. Ibid., p. 160.

73. Joyce Nelson, *The Perfect Machine — Television and the Bomb,* New Society Publishers, Phila., PA, 1992, p. 145.

74. Ibid., p. 146.

75. Father Frank Poncelet, *Air Waves From Hell,* The Newman Press, Long Prairie, MN, 1992, p. 205.

The important writing you have just read will convict and change society. Our goals must be to spread these truths. I SEE FAR_™, originally printed in the Community of Caritas of Birmingham newsletter, is now being made available in book form at a price in volume discount in order for you to permeate society with the truth, in order to change it. You may order in discounted volume to give to a friend, spouse, children, or give away at churches and conferences.

You may purchase this book at your local bookstore. If they do not have it, please ask them to order it. In that way, distribution will spread and many more will be led to Our Lady's plans to change the world through the family.

Buy at your local bookstore. If not available, you may order from:

Caritas of Birmingham
100 Our Lady Queen of Peace Drive
Sterrett, AL 35147 USA

or call 205-672-2000, ext. 315.

You may use Visa, Mastercard, or Discover to order.

I See Far™ BF104		
(Check One)		
❏ 1	$6.00	
❏ 5	$20.00	($4.00EA)
❏ 10	$30.00	($3.00EA)
❏ 25	$47.50	($1.90EA)
❏ 50	$90.00	($1.80EA)
❏ 100	$170.00	($1.70EA)
❏ 1000	$1400.00	($1.40EA)

Shipping & Handling		
Order Sub-total	U.S. Mail (Standard)	UPS (Faster)
$0-$10.00	$5.00	$9.00
$10.01-$20.00	$7.50	$11.50
$20.01-$50.00	$10.00	$14.00
$50.01-$100.00	$15.00	$19.00
Over $100.00	15% of total	18% of total

For overnight delivery, call for pricing.
***International (Surface):**
Double above shipping Cost.
Call for faster International delivery.

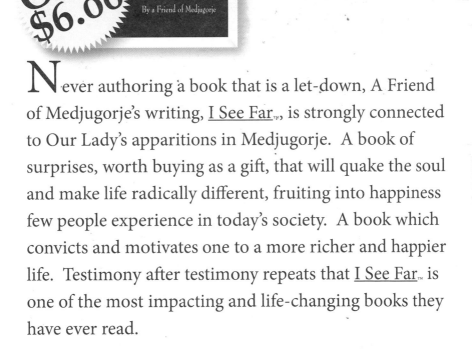

Never authoring a book that is a let-down, A Friend of Medjugorje's writing, <u>I See Far</u>™, is strongly connected to Our Lady's apparitions in Medjugorje. A book of surprises, worth buying as a gift, that will quake the soul and make life radically different, fruiting into happiness few people experience in today's society. A book which convicts and motivates one to a more richer and happier life. Testimony after testimony repeats that <u>I See Far</u>™ is one of the most impacting and life-changing books they have ever read.

Buy at your local bookstore.
Or call 205-672-2000 ext. 315 (24 hr)

The book that has changed and saved
thousands of marriages around the world.

How to Change
Your
Husband.

Owner's Manual for the Family
By a Friend of Medjugorje

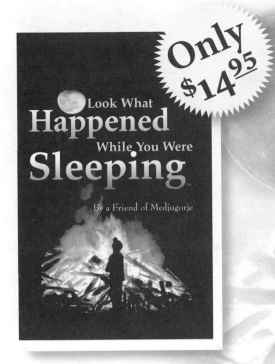

6/4/2007
"Thank you so much for recommending all of us who read this webpage tonight at Ivan's apparition. That was so very, very thoughtful and beautiful to do. I feel "touched" in a special way this evening. God Bless All!!! THANK YOU. THANK YOU."

M.C.
Middletown, New Jersey – USA

6/11/2007
"Just looking at the pictures, I can feel the presence of Our Lady…"

D.S.
La Grange, Texas – USA

6/5/2007
"Now I can receive Our Lady's messages faster and everything else that is happening in Medjugorje and Caritas sooner."

J.H.
Boalsburg, Pennsylvania – USA

6/5/2007
"Every time I read the recent message and look at the photos, on mej.com, I feel as if I am right back there with all of you. Thank you for sharing these experiences…"

Wisconsin, – USA

Check out
www.mej.com
and sign up for it's free mailing list.

Growing everyday as the most extensive Medjugorje website in the world.